WHEN LOVE REMAINS

RHONDA DIMARTINO

Copyright Page

When Love Remains
A Novel by Rhonda DiMartino

ISBN: 978-1-83556-483-7 - eBook
ISBN: 978-1-83556-484-4 - Paperback
ISBN: 978-1-83556-485-1 - Hardback

Cover design and artwork © Rhonda DiMartino
Printed in the United States of America
First Edition, 2025

Dedication

For the boy who walked beside me through the shadows, who held my hand when I thought I couldn't go on, who became my reason to rise each morning. You grew wiser than your years, carrying burdens no child should ever have to carry, and yet you did so with grace, strength, and love that gave me hope when I had none.

For the man whose love shaped me, whose absence carved an ache so deep that even time will never fully ease the pain. You were my safe place, my steady ground, the one who showed me the beauty of ordinary days. Though you are gone, your presence still lingers in every quiet moment, in the lessons you left behind, and in the love that continues to guide us forward.

For the man who came after, whose love arrived like light breaking through a storm. You showed me that laughter could return, that passion could be reborn, that healing was possible. You have been patient with my grief, tender with my heart, and steadfast in your devotion — reminding me that even after loss, love can rise again, stronger and deeper than I ever imagined.

And for the woman who first believed in me, who saw something in my words long before I did. You nurtured my dreams, encouraged my voice, and loved me in a way that still carries me. Even now, I can feel your pride. Even now, you remain my quiet anchor.
This book is for all of you — my greatest heartbreak, my greatest blessing, my greatest hope, and my first believer. You are in every page, every breath, every piece of who I am. Without you, there would be no story. Without your love, I would never be who or where I am today.

Thank you. I love you always.

CONTENTS

FOREWORD

This story is not my story – Not exactly.

But it was born from the deepest places of my heart — from the quiet ache of grief, from the fierce love of a mother, and from the hollow space left behind when the person you built your life with suddenly vanishes from it.

When Love Remains was inspired by what it means to lose a soulmate. Not just the pain of absence, but the unbearable silence that follows. The weight of carrying on, not just for yourself, but for the child who still looks to you for answers, for strength, for hope. Writing this book was a way for me to hold a mirror to my own sorrow — and then to ask what comes next.

In this semi-fictional tale, Rainey loses her husband suddenly, and in the aftermath, she must navigate the impossible: learning to breathe again, to feel again, to open herself up to a world that no longer feels safe. Her journey is not identical to mine, but the emotions that carry her — the guilt, the longing, the fierce protectiveness of a child left behind, and the slow, terrifying emergence of desire — are ones I know intimately.

This is a love story, but not the kind that begins with fireworks and flirtation. This is the kind that begins in the ruins. The kind that asks: Is there still life left in me? Could someone love the broken parts? And if they do... will I let them?

Love after loss doesn't arrive in grand declarations — it arrives in safety, presence, and quiet truth. That's the kind of love this book explores. One that honors what came before, while still daring to reach for what might come next.

— Rhonda DiMartino

AUBURN

Chapter One

THE ABYSS

Rainey

The worst part about flying wasn't the turbulence, or the crying babies, or even the recycled air.

It was the memories.

It had been one year, eleven months, and thirteen days since she boarded a plane. And she remembered every second of the last one — screaming for help in a hotel room in New Orleans, her husband's eyes wide and unblinking as she pressed down on his chest, again and again, hearing nothing but the whisper of her own voice piecing together frantic prayers from her trembling lips.

Shane was forty-three.

Athletic. Strong. Smiling one minute. Dead the next.

She had given him CPR for eighteen minutes while her son watched.

Eighteen minutes of begging.
Eighteen minutes of sweat, terror, wailing, agony, and disbelief.

When the paramedics arrived, she was still shivering and drenched in her own tears. As they pulled her off of him, she'd collapsed while staff, other hotel guests, and total strangers stood by and witnessed the most traumatic and defining moment in her life.

She had spent the next three months in a fog.

Not a gentle, drifting mist — but the kind that settles deep into your lungs, thick and choking. Her brain refused to hold a thought for more than ten seconds at a time. Friends came. Neighbors dropped off food. The funeral was planned. Someone must have chosen a casket. Someone picked the flowers and the music.

But she remembered none of it.

Grief had turned her into a ghost.

She moved through her house like a haunted woman, unable to sit still yet incapable of doing anything useful. She kept opening drawers and forgetting why. She'd pour a cup of coffee and leave it on the stairs. She'd wake in the middle of the night convinced Shane was in the shower, and walk toward the sound of water only to remember her son had started showering twice a day because it was the only place he could cry.

Dillon.

God, that boy.

He was twelve.

He had been the one to call 911.
He had followed the dispatcher's instructions like a soldier, steady and calm.

He hadn't cried until two days later, when he walked into their home and saw Shane's baseball glove still on the counter.

That night, she crawled into his bed and held him until they both passed out.
They did that a lot after Shane died — held each other to keep from disappearing.

Now, nearly two years later, she sat stiff and hollow at Gate C11, holding a paper cup of coffee she couldn't bring herself to drink.

She was wearing Shane's old college sweatshirt — washed a few times since he died, but it still carried the faintest trace of him. Now, it also smelled like Dillon, because he'd worn it a thousand times since that awful day.

She had considered changing before leaving the house. She had picked up a soft cashmere cardigan — more flattering, more refined — but this was the only thing that felt like armor.

Everything else made her feel exposed.

The woman she used to be — the warm, magnetic, laugh-too-loud Rainey — had been buried with Shane.

She exhaled slowly, watching the terminal fill with people.

Business travelers. Distracted mothers. Someone loudly FaceTiming near a vending machine.

All of them had destinations.

She had none.

Just movement. Just an ache so constant it had started to feel like a second skin. Not pain exactly. Something quieter. Numb, but tender. Like a bruise she couldn't stop pressing.

Her phone buzzed.

Dillon: You okay?

Her lips twitched.

Rainey: Still breathing. You okay?

Dillon: Yes. You've got this, Mom. I'm proud of you.

She stared at his words. Let them sink in.

"We've got this."

> *Those three little words. Rainey remembers hiding in the bedroom closet one week after the funeral, knees drawn to her chest, wailing and shaking so hard she could barely breathe. Dillon found her.*
> *He didn't cry. He didn't panic.*
> *He sat beside her and wrapped his arms tightly around her entire body.*
> *He whispered, "We've got this. I promise. I love you so much, Mom." His voice had cracked. His hands shaking when he found hers. But he held on anyway.*

He was proud of her.
Even after everything he'd seen.

He had grown noticeably taller in the last year. His voice had deepened. But it wasn't puberty that changed him — it was grief. Grief had aged him. Matured him. Made him fiercely protective of her.

And she loved him for it. Love beyond any unit of measurement. But it also broke her heart.

He shouldn't have to worry about his mother surviving each day. Not whether she remembered to eat. Not whether she had the strength to comb the tangles from her hair. Not whether she was "okay enough" to drive.

He should be thinking about baseball, girls, homework, and how to sneak online to play video games after curfew.

The boarding call crackled overhead, startling her out of her spiral.

Group One, now boarding.

Rainey stood slowly. Her body ached in places that had nothing to do with age. She was only forty-six, but she moved like someone much older — cautious, deliberate, guarded.

"Mom."

She turned.

Dillon stood just beyond the roped-off line, hoodie pulled low over his eyes. His backpack slung over one shoulder. He was still her sweet boy — but looking more like a man every time she blinked. Like someone who had already lived through the most unimaginable catastrophe and stood firm with a coat of resilience.

"You sure about this?" he asked, his voice low, but steady.

"No," she admitted.

He smiled. "That's okay. Do it anyway."

She moved toward him and wrapped her arms around his tall frame, squeezing tightly.

He hugged her back without hesitation. He had the grip of a man twice his size.

"You know how strong you are?" she whispered.

He shrugged. "You're stronger."

"Not even close."

He pulled back just enough to look her in the eye.

"You're the strongest person I've ever met, Mom."

Tears threatened, but she blinked them away. "Promise me you'll text me if you need anything."

"I will. But you're the one flying solo, remember?"

She laughed, a short, cracked sound. "Don't remind me."

He pulled his phone out. "One more selfie."

She groaned. "I look awful."

"You look beautiful," he said, as he had a million times.

And he meant it.

His mom was full of love, strength, grace — and all of the qualities that made him simply adore her.

They leaned together, cheek to cheek. The photo snapped.

Then, he kissed her forehead.

"You got this," he said. "I'll be here when you get back."

And then, just like that, he was gone — disappearing into the crowd of waiting parents and noisy travelers.

Rainey turned toward the gate and stepped forward, one trembling foot at a time.

She didn't know where this trip would take her.
Only that staying might finally kill her.

She had been dying inside for so long now, and as much as she loved Dillon, she felt completely alone in the world.

The plane was half-full.

She took her window seat and stared out at the gray tarmac, her body coiled like wire. Her fingers clenched the armrest even before the engines started.

Her breath came too shallow. She counted to four, in and out, trying to slow her pulse.

It didn't help.

She hadn't been kissed in nearly two years.

That realization hit her suddenly, stupidly — like the thought had just been sitting in the back of her brain, waiting to be noticed.

She missed being kissed.
Held.
Desired.
Even flirted with.

> *Shane had a habit of touching her when no one was looking — brushing the back of her neck in grocery lines, sliding his palm across her waist while cooking, whispering something filthy and sweet in her ear before dinner guests arrived. Cradling her to sleep every night.*
> *They made love every Sunday morning. Not out of routine — but reverence. And afterward, they'd sip coffee on the porch, her feet in his lap, talking about everything and nothing.*
> *Spoiled. Cherished. She was **loved**.*

Now, it felt like a sin to want that again.

To *need* it.

She turned her face toward the window and shut her eyes.

She didn't want to think anymore.
She didn't want to *feel*.

And that's when she felt him.

A shift in the air.

A pull — low in her belly and unmistakably real.

She opened her eyes and turned her head.

And there he was.

Sitting across the aisle and one row forward. Facing straight ahead. Still as stone.

He didn't look at her.

But she couldn't stop looking at him.

Tall. Broad. Immense.

His gray hoodie stretched across thick shoulders, and his jeans fit snug across powerful thighs. He had strong arms — she could tell even from the way they rested casually against the armrest. His hands were large, tan, and scarred, with veins that ran like rivers across his knuckles.

And then there was his face.

Chiseled. Unapologetic. A strong jaw, lightly peppered with salt and shadow. Thick brows. His hair was dark, streaked with silver at the temples.

Not styled. Not forced. Just... worn.

Lived-in.

Like the rest of him.

And those eyes.

God, those eyes.

Even without looking at her, they made her feel *seen*.

She noticed the clip on his waistband. A glint of metal. A badge.

Air Marshal.

Of course.

He wasn't just any man.

He was methodical. Trained. A wall with legs. And yet... there was something in the way he sat. Something in the way he breathed, like the world around him didn't touch him anymore. Like he'd already seen the worst of it.

And survived.

She turned away quickly, cheeks warm.

Her heart pounded against her ribs like it was trying to escape.

What the hell was that?

She hadn't reacted like that to anyone in years.

She peeked again.

He hadn't moved.

Still calm.
Still unreadable.
Still unaware — or so it seemed.

But she *felt* him.

She could feel him.

And something deep inside her — a part she thought had been buried with Shane — stirred awake.

Chapter Two

TURBULENCE

Jake

ake Walker didn't believe in fate.

He believed in patterns. In instincts. In reading a room, scanning a crowd, watching for the stutter-step or the wrong breath or the quick glance that meant trouble.

That's what had kept him alive.
And it's what made him very, very good at his job.

So when he first felt her presence — before even seeing her — he didn't label it as fate.

He labeled it as a shift.

A subtle rearranging of the air around him.
Like something had entered the equation and refused to blend.

She stepped onto the plane like she was walking into a war zone.

Eyes lowered. Shoulders stiff. Movements tight.

Not afraid. Not frantic.

Just... frayed.

Like a woman who'd been unraveled and stitched herself back together in a rush.
Sloppy seams. Still bleeding beneath.

He watched her without watching her. Peripheral. Strategic.

She didn't notice him.

People rarely did.

He'd spent years perfecting the art of invisibility — blending in, observing without being seen. It was a skill he relied on in dark places. In alleys behind consulates. On tarmacs in the Middle East. On a dozen flights a month.

The badge on his waistband was tucked beneath a gray hoodie. His jeans were loose, plain. His boots scuffed but quiet. He looked like anyone. And that was the point.

He clocked her seat: 11A. Window. Diagonal from his own.

He didn't mean to check the flight manifest.
He really didn't.

But he did.

DeMarco, Rainey.

The name caught in his throat like a sliver of glass.

It sounded classic. Almost elegant. Like someone who once had monogrammed stationery and a passport with too many stamps. But there was a softness to it too. Rainey. Not something tight around the edges.

Rainey.

Like water.

Like grief.

He didn't intend to keep looking.

But he did.

Not in a way that would set off alarms. Just quick glances. A scan of posture. Of hands. Of breath.

She was beautiful. No question.

But not in a polished, manicured way.

She looked like someone who had once cared — a woman who wore perfume and matching earrings and remembered the names of waiters — but who had stopped somewhere along the line. Not out of laziness, but out of heartbreak.

Her beauty wasn't deliberate. It leaked out of her despite the sorrow.

Her hands rested still in her lap. No phone. No earbuds. Just stillness.

Too much of it.

Jake shifted in his seat and exhaled slowly.

He wasn't a man who felt much these days. He was comfortable in the cold. It made him effective.

Distance was survival. Emotion got people killed.

That's what he'd learned early — in the military, in the marshals, in marriage, in courtrooms, and in sterile hospital rooms where things beeped until they didn't.

He didn't do intimacy anymore.

The women he slept with understood that. They came to him for the quiet. The control. The rough hands that didn't shake. The illusion of stability.

When they asked for more, he disappeared.

Clean. Quick. Detached.

His last relationship — if you could call it that — ended after four months when she told him he was a locked door and she was tired of knocking.

Good, he'd thought.

He liked his doors locked.

Locked meant safe.

Locked meant no one got hurt — least of all him.

But Rainey...

She was a déjà vu made of longing.

Soft. Storm-washed. Stunning.

He noticed the indentation on her left hand. The phantom wedding band.

He assessed. She'd been through hell. A bitter divorce? The death of a husband? Something. The grief engulfed her from head to toe, and the way she moved — as though still walking through water — made his chest feel tight.

She flinched when the captain announced a delay.

Not visibly. Just a flicker — a snag in her breath. A tiny shudder.

Like one more inconvenience might snap the last thread she was holding.

Jake's hands curled into fists.

Not in anger.

In awareness.

That kind of woman wasn't someone you just noticed.

She was someone you felt.

And he felt her.

In his chest.
In his gut.
And, damn it — lower than that, too.

He adjusted in his seat, annoyed with his body.

This wasn't about sex. It couldn't be.
She had complication written all over her in permanent ink.

But her scent — something warm and clean and faintly floral — had drifted across the narrow aisle and made a home in his lungs.

Her hair shimmered in the dull cabin light. Thick and golden.

He imagined the feel of it twisted in his fingers.

No.

He shut that down hard.

This was a flight.
A job.
A moment.

Nothing more.

He forced himself to go blank.

Counted backwards from one hundred.
A trick from his early deployments.

He was at sixty-two when the plane jolted from turbulence.

His head snapped instinctively toward her.

She hadn't moved.

No startle. No flinch.
Just a slow, deep breath — her eyes closed, her jaw set.

Resigned.

Jake frowned.

The idea that she didn't react to sudden movement — didn't even blink — bothered him more than it should've.

She was used to chaos. That much was clear.

But something about it... stirred the protective part of him.

Not chivalry.
Not instinct.

Code.

That ancient wiring that made him want to stand between her and the world.

Shield her.
Watch her back.
Keep her breathing.

He'd only ever felt that for teammates and blood.

Not strangers.

And never women.

That kind of attachment was dangerous.
It blurred the line.
It got people killed.

He turned his eyes back to the aisle.

Forced himself to forget the shape of her mouth.

She shifted slightly in her seat, and Jake saw it — the way her shoulders curled inward, like she was trying to take up less space in a world that had already taken too much from her. There was a quiet fragility about her, not weakness, but something worn thin.

Something tender.

And it did something to him.
Something sharp.
Something aching.

Because in that small, unspoken moment, he realized he couldn't remember the last time he'd touched someone with softness — not out of duty, not out of instinct, but with wounded gentleness.

He'd held pressure points, braced bodies, carried weight.
But placid affection — tender, unguarded, and unearned —
that was a language he hadn't spoken in years.

And just watching her — silent, bruised by life, holding herself together with invisible thread —
he found himself wanting to speak it again.

He leaned his head against the wall and closed his eyes.

Images flooded — not of her body, but her grief. Her silence. Her restraint.

He wanted to know what broke her.

And what held her together.

He wanted to ask her when she'd last slept through the night. If she still reached for someone in her dreams. If she could stand silence. If she could stand music. If she ever found herself laughing and felt ashamed for it.

He wanted to ask her if she was running from something or to something.

But that wasn't his place.

Not today.

Not ever.

Still, when the plane began to descend and the city lights blurred beneath them like scattered embers, Jake turned his head.

Rainey

She stared out the window, her fingers pressed lightly against her lips.

She leaned into the pane and stared into the clouds as they slowly escaped. There was something sacred about being up here — above the noise, above the ache. And suddenly she imagined him in the same seat, some flight years ago, staring out into the same endless sky and thinking of her. Of Dillon.

> *Shane's work saw him traveling often in the last three years of his life. He flew across time zones and continents — China, Germany, Dubai — places they once circled on maps during long-ago date nights, dreaming of "someday." Back then, it felt like too much. But now?*
>
> *Now it felt like a gift.*
>
> *He'd seen the world. He'd stood in cities he once only read about, eaten food he could barely pronounce, smiled at strangers in foreign markets, and sent her blurry pictures and videos from street corners halfway around the globe.*

She closed her eyes.

> *Did he still see them?*
>
> *Was he out there somewhere, just beyond the clouds, trying to tell them he was okay?*

The thought wasn't rational. She knew that. But grief didn't need to be rational to be real.

> *Sometimes, in the quiet hours of the night — just before sleep or just after a nightmare — she swore she could feel him near. Like the air shifted, or the temperature dropped. Like her heart reached out and brushed something invisible. Something that resonated **him**.*
>
> *Maybe the world he lived in now wasn't so far.*
>
> *Maybe love didn't end. It just... changed altitude.*

She wasn't crying.
She wasn't even blinking.

Just holding it in.

He admired that.
And hated it.

Because holding it in meant she'd probably done it for too long.

And then, for the first time, she looked at him.

Not accidentally.

Not a glance.

A look.

Direct. Open. Long enough to notice the flecks of green in her irises. Long enough for the corner of her mouth to twitch — not a smile, not quite — just... acknowledgment.

Recognition.

Jake felt something shift again.

And everything in him went quiet.

Chapter Three

GROUNDED

Rainey

The plane landed with a soft thud and a dull, collective sigh from the cabin. The familiar rattle of overhead bins opening, seatbelts snapping, and restless passengers preparing to stampede broke the fragile silence she had wrapped herself in like a cocoon.

Shane had always been the one with the plan. Precise. Methodical. Whether it was balancing their finances or mapping out the perfect vacation, he handled everything with care and intention. She used to joke that her only job was to pack a bag and show up — he'd already done the rest.

They used to dream aloud about the places they'd go once life slowed down. Italy. France. Thailand. China. New Zealand. That was just the beginning of their list, scribbled on napkins and tucked into notebooks over the years. They wanted to walk through vineyards in Tuscany, eat street food in Bangkok, and wake up in a cottage on the South Island with nothing on the agenda but each other.

But life had other plans. They'd poured so much of themselves into building their business in the early years, then into the career he took on afterward, that time just kept slipping away. There were always deadlines. Always responsibilities. Vacations were postponed. Postcards were never written. And in the end, they never got to take even half the trips they promised each other they would.

Yet here she was. She didn't move.

Rainey sat stoically, hands resting on her thighs, heart still beating too fast. She wasn't sure if it was the descent that rattled her or the man sitting across the aisle and one row ahead.

Jake

He didn't move.

Let her stand first.

Her hair brushed his arm.

She smelled like memory.

Like spring mornings on back porches. Like hope that hadn't died yet.

She turned slightly.

Their eyes met once more.

And in that instant — barely three seconds long — Jake Walker realized he hadn't been a ghost in someone's story for so long, he'd forgotten what it felt like to be seen.

Not sized up.
Not scanned for threat.

Seen.

And for the first time in years, the locked door inside him… clicked.

She knew his name now. He'd said it to her, low and simple, like it didn't matter. But it did. It had echoed in her chest ever since.

Jake.

There was something about the way the sound filled her head - grounded, masculine, final. A name that fit him like a worn leather holster. Unpolished but strong. And just a little dangerous.

She hadn't meant to engage him after the flight. She hadn't planned to speak to anyone. Her trip was supposed to be quiet. Low-key. She wasn't ready to be seen…not like this. Not with her grief so visible, so close to the surface it threatened to spill out if she made the wrong kind of eye contact.

But then he'd appeared.

Strong. Silent. Watching the world with a predator's patience.

He had looked at her like he already knew.

Not who she was, but what she was: a woman barely held together by willpower and obligations.

And somehow, she hadn't looked away.

That was the part she couldn't stop replaying.

The way her gaze had locked with his at the gate. At baggage claim. That moment when his fingers brushed hers as he reached across — so minor, so stupid — but the spark had been real.

And it scared her.

Not because she wasn't ready.

But because some hidden, aching part of her had been *starving*.

She followed the line of passengers out of the terminal, dragging her suitcase behind her like it weighed more than it should. She wasn't meeting anyone. She hadn't told anyone she was coming except Dillon. This trip was for her.

She told herself that again, as if repeating it would make it feel true.

But her skin still tingled from that brief contact. From his voice. From the way his eyes lingered like he wasn't afraid of the quiet between them.

She reached the curb, her head swimming.

The air was damp and heavy with drizzle. A hotel shuttle was idling by the sidewalk. She walked toward it, dazed, distracted.

And that's when she turned.

She didn't know why she did it. Instinct, maybe. Or that unshakable pull.

Jake was standing inside the terminal, behind the glass doors. Just standing. Watching her.

He didn't move.

Neither did she.

For a second, the world blurred. The cars, the people, the noise — all faded to gray.

And then she turned away, heart hammering, and stepped into the shuttle.

The hotel room was small, but clean. Soft yellow light spilled from the lamps, giving everything a kind of golden softness. The king bed was covered in too many pillows, the way she liked. And the desk still smelled faintly of furniture polish. She inhaled, the scent yanking her back in time like a hand on her chest.

Shane used to jokingly tease for her obsession with bed pillows, "Why does anyone need this many?" — before tossing three to the floor and pulling her into his arms like gravity had just doubled.

She could still picture him standing in their bedroom, freshly showered, wrapped in a towel. The sounds of his voice barely a whisper now – but preserved in kept voicemails.

She sank onto the edge of the bed, her fingers grazing the comforter like it still held the shape of him — the warmth he left behind, still lingering.

Tears prickled behind her eyes, but she didn't blink them away.

She let them come.

Because in this space, with the soft lamplight and that phantom scent of lemon and lavender, she could almost pretend he was still there — just in the bathroom brushing his teeth, or pulling the covers down with that sleepy grin, about to ask her to come curl up beside him.

But the room was still.

And he was gone.

Rainey set her bag down and sank into the chair near the window. She didn't even take off her coat. Just stared out into the misty city skyline.

Her hands were still trembling.

It wasn't just Jake's presence that haunted her - it was her *reaction* to him. The way her body had betrayed her. The warmth in her belly. The slow ache that had bloomed between her thighs and spread like honey.

She hadn't felt that in years.

Not since Shane.

And even then... it had never struck this fast. This hard.

Jake hadn't touched her. Hadn't flirted. Hadn't said anything suggestive.

But it didn't matter.

His eyes had undressed her.

Not crudely. Not like a man who wanted to conquer her body.

No, he'd looked at her like a man who wanted to own every broken piece of her.

She curled up in the chair, knees drawn to her chest, forehead resting on the edge of the cushion.

She hated herself for how much she wanted to feel that again.

To be *wanted*. Not gently. Not kindly. But *claimed*.

It was shameful. Irrational. She didn't know him.

And yet she'd felt safer in his presence than she had in two years.

Even the air had changed when he was near - heavier, charged, like the pressure before a storm.

She hadn't been *moved* since Shane died.

She hadn't let anyone that close. And even when she tried, it all felt empty.

Dillon had needed her. Her friends and family had pulled back, unsure how to speak to the grieving widow. And her body had become a monument to loss; something to maintain, not enjoy.

But Jake... Jake made her remember.

She stood, stripped off her coat, and padded into the bathroom.

The mirror was unforgiving. Lines beneath her eyes. A faint crease between her brows. Her mouth still had fullness, but her expression had aged since Shane's death. It was subtler than time. It was grief.

She turned on the water and splashed her face.

Then she stared at herself for a long time.

Her skin still remembered how it felt to be held. Her mouth still ached for something deeper than silence. And her thighs... they throbbed with a ghost hunger she hadn't expected.

She didn't want to think about sex. It felt wrong.

But she couldn't stop thinking about him.

How his hands would feel if they ever held her face.

How his weight would feel above her.

How it would feel to *surrender* to someone again - not because she was weak, but because she was tired of being the strong one.

She leaned against the sink, heart pounding.

She couldn't go down this road. She wasn't ready.

And yet... she wasn't sure she could stop it either.

Not if he looked at her like that again.

Not if he said her name like it mattered.

Not if she let herself believe that maybe-just maybe-there was still something inside her worth claiming.

Chapter Four

REACTIVATED

Jake

He told himself to walk away.

He'd done his part. Didn't intrude. Said his name. Didn't linger too long. Didn't make her uncomfortable.

And yet here he was, thirty feet from the baggage carousel, standing dead still with his hands in his pockets, watching her like she was a loose thread in his reality. Something unspooling slowly. Something he needed to understand.

She hadn't spoken much. Barely even looked at him after that brief connection in the terminal.

But he couldn't stop looking at her.

And that? That scared the hell out of him.

She didn't dress like a woman who wanted to be noticed. Worn jeans. Oversized sweatshirt. Minimal makeup. Hair unstyled but somehow still elegant. The kind of beauty that wasn't performed—it just was.

But it was her stillness that got him.

Jake had spent his life reading people. Six years in the Air Force. Thirteen more with the Air Marshal Service. Before that? Security contracts overseas—war zones, diplomatic details, cartel extraction. He'd seen terror. Fury. Panic. He knew how to clock it in a second.

But grief? Grief was quieter.

And that woman radiated it in waves.

Her son's face had flashed through Jake's mind the moment she said the word "grief." It wasn't conscious. It was instinct.

He'd seen that expression before—on a boy's face in Kandahar. Eight years old. Eyes too old for his face and a body too small for his age. Standing over a father in the dirt. Silent. Motionless. Not crying. Just watching.

Jake had carried that boy out under fire. The kid hadn't said a word. Not one. But he'd gripped Jake's vest like it was the last real thing left in the world.

That's what grief did to people. It froze them. Crystallized them. And if they weren't careful, they never melted again.

It was why Jake had finally chosen to step off the battlefield for good—not with fanfare, but with the quiet ache of a man who'd seen enough. His contract was up, but the truth ran deeper than paperwork. He'd served his country, carried the weight, watched too many lives break in front of him. And now, after this last flight, he wasn't just going home. He was choosing something rarer than duty—peace.

The luggage carousel churned to life. Jake's bag rolled out quickly. He grabbed it, but didn't move.

Across the terminal, Rainey—God, even her name had stuck in his throat like a memory—stood near the far wall. Watching the bags rotate. Her posture hadn't changed. Still upright. Still poised. But she wasn't there. Not fully.

She looked like a woman suspended in time. Like she'd forgotten how to take up space.

Jake told himself again: Walk away.

But he didn't.

Instead, he watched.

She picked up her roller bag slowly, as if even that small task required deliberation. Her phone buzzed—he saw the flash of light against her hip—but she didn't check it.

She just adjusted the strap of her purse and turned toward the exit.

Jake followed.

He didn't mean to. He wasn't chasing her. He just… moved.

Feet on autopilot. Mind running static.

She exited through the glass doors. He caught the last glimpse of her hair as it disappeared into the overcast light. Rain had started. Barely a drizzle. Just enough to blur edges and soak collars.

Outside, taxis crawled along the curb. A few travelers cursed the cold.

Rainey stood near a hotel shuttle. The driver was tossing bags into the rear compartment.

She looked over her shoulder—just briefly.

Her eyes locked with his through the glass.

And something in Jake's chest moved. Shifted like plates under the surface.

She didn't smile. Didn't nod.

But she saw him.

She got into the van. The door slid shut. The shuttle pulled away.

Jake stood there with his pulse in his ears and no idea what the hell he was doing.

Ten minutes later, he was home.

He dropped his bag by the dresser and stood in the middle of the living room, hands on his hips, breathing hard for no reason at all.

She was gone.

Good.

That was good.

He didn't need another woman threading herself into his blood—especially now. For the first time in decades, his time was his own. No flight rosters. No briefings. No missions. He could wake up in the mountains or fall asleep near the sea. Eat cold Spam out of a can or order the best damn steak he could find. It didn't matter. No one was waiting. No one was asking. He belonged to no one—and for better or worse, that kind of freedom could make a man forget how to be needed.

He wandered through to the kitchen, then reached into the fridge and grabbed a bottled water. Before even realizing it, he was on the edge of his bed. Staring at the blank TV screen.

His phone vibrated…Work?

Text from Richards: "Debrief call moved to 0800. Team dinner optional tonight. Stay sharp."

Jake didn't respond.

He wasn't going. Apparently they hadn't removed him from the group messages, or maybe they just assumed he couldn't *really* walk away.

He didn't want to talk to anyone. Didn't want to listen to shallow jokes or pretend to care about the rookie's first arrest. He just didn't care anymore.

He stood and walked to the window.

The rain came down harder now, blurring the city. Headlights smeared against the glass like oil paints.

He pressed his forehead to the cool pane.

Rainey.

He said her name again in his head, as if that would settle something. As if it would loosen the knot forming in his chest.

What the hell had she done to him?

He didn't believe in soulmates. That was fantasy. He believed in broken people finding each other for warmth, then walking away once the fire died.

But this didn't feel like warmth.

This felt like heat.

Not just sexual, though. Hell, the way her mouth moved when she said his name... it made his hands itch.

No. This was different.

This was pull. This was gravity.

He saw something in her that mirrored the worst parts of himself. The hollow parts. The parts no one ever bothered to ask about. And he hadn't even spoken ten words to her.

He dragged a hand over his face.

Get your shit together.

He had six kids. Six. Scattered, raised by women who outgrew him, who resented him, who left before he had the chance to leave first. He loved his kids, sure. But love was never enough. He barely knew who they were anymore.

He'd screwed it up. All of it. Every relationship. Every chance at something lasting.

So what was he even thinking? Rainey wasn't a one-night fix. She wasn't a comfort. She was a storm. Soft but fierce. And if he wasn't careful, she'd drown him.

He showered. Scrubbed himself raw. Stood under scalding water like it could boil her out of his head.

Then he lay down on what felt like the stiffest mattress of his life, alone, wide awake, wondering if she was out there on the edge of a bed just like this... thinking about him too.

He dozed sometime after 2 a.m.

And that's when the dream came.

Not violent. Not overtly sexual. Just... vivid.

He was standing in an open field, the tall grass brushing against his legs like whispers. The wind moved through everything — restless, alive.

And in the distance, she appeared.

Rainey.

Barefoot.

Still.

Wearing a sheer white dress that clung to the lines of her body and fluttered around her thighs like smoke.

She wasn't smiling.

Just watching him — with eyes that didn't blink, didn't waver.

Like she saw something in him he hadn't yet found in himself.

He tried to move toward her, but his feet sank in the earth like cement.

She tilted her head, eyes soft but sad.

Then she turned and walked away.

He jolted awake as though breaking through deep water, breathless and disoriented. Sheets tangled. Sweat cold on his chest.

He sat up, breath catching, hand fisting against his knee.

Outside, the city hadn't changed. But something inside him had.

And he wasn't sure he could change it back.

Chapter Five

THE STORM

Rainey

The rain had stopped by morning, but the sky was still gray. Not the soft, cloudy kind — the bruised kind. The kind that pressed against your chest, heavy with things unsaid.

Shane loved the rain. He used to say it made everything feel alive — the earth, the air, even him. When they moved from Colorado, it was all he talked about that first week. He stood barefoot in the backyard, arms stretched toward the sky like he was summoning it, laughing as he imagined the first real southern storm.
But the rain didn't come.
Texas stayed dry. The air was hot and still.

And Shane died in that drought.

Three weeks after they arrived. Eight days after Dillon walked nervously into a brand-new school with unfamiliar hallways and no friends….His dad. Her husband. Gone. He collapsed in that damn hotel room, and the skies screamed with paralyzing silence. But after the funeral — after the chaos, the casseroles, the quiet — the heavens finally opened. And it poured. For five days straight. A rain unlike any they'd seen.
Like the sky was mourning with them.
Like it waited until they couldn't take the dryness anymore.

And in some strange, sacred way, it felt like Shane had called it down. As if his soul had broken through the clouds and wept with them — not from sorrow, but from knowing just how deeply he was loved.

Rainey stood at the window of her hotel room, barefoot, coffee untouched in her hand. She hadn't slept well. Or maybe she had, but the dreams had left her shaken and warm in places that made her ashamed.

She didn't dream of Shane anymore – not because she didn't' *want* to, but because she *couldn't*.

She used to - in the early days, every night. She would see him smiling, or standing at the foot of their bed, or reaching for her across a wide, impossible room. Sometimes he was whole. Sometimes just a shadow.

Now?

Now her mind gave her Jake.

She'd seen him in sleep: holding her wrists above her head, whispering her name like a warning. In the dream, she hadn't resisted. She'd offered herself. Not as a desperate woman seeking comfort, but as something deliberate. She'd wanted to be taken. Completely. And the way he looked at her...

That look still burned under her skin.

Rainey pressed her palm against the cool glass. The city moved beneath her - strangers walking fast with umbrellas, taxis honking. People LIVING because their entire lives hadn't shattered in one departing breath.

She wondered where he was. Jake.

That name shouldn't carry weight. But it did.

Where are you right now?
Are you thinking about me?

She shook the thoughts from her head.

This was foolish. She didn't know him. Not really. But her body didn't care. Her body remembered how his presence had altered the air. How safe and exposed she'd felt in the exact same moment. How his voice had slipped under her skin like a current.

And the worst part?

She wanted more.

Not just sex, though. God, yes! She wanted that, too. But also the quiet. The certainty. The stillness he carried like armor. He looked like a man who could take a woman's burdens and never flinch.

And she had so many burdens.

She turned away from the window, heart fluttering with something between guilt and hunger.

She thought of Dillon.

He had texted her again last night - just a heart emoji and a photo of the dog curled up on the couch. He was good. Steady. Funny. Wise in many ways she didn't understand, but even wiser in ways she hated that she did.

And he loved her. Fiercely.

He didn't want her to be alone.

"Mom, my friend's dad is really nice. I think you'd like him. He owns a car dealership, and he's been single for a long time..."

*It had been nearly a year since Shane's death—and that was the first time she truly **yelled** at Dillon. The suggestion hit her like a betrayal, not because Dillon meant harm, but because the very idea of another man stepping into the sacred space she and Shane had built felt like sacrilege. The thought of replacing Shane—especially coming from their own son—devastated her. She and Shane hadn't just been married; they had become **one**. It was the three of them against the world. And now, the idea that someone else could simply fill that void felt impossible.*

*She despised herself for snapping at him. Dillon was grieving too, and he didn't just want her to be happy again—he **needed** it, in the way only a child clings to the hope that their parent might someday* *smile like they used to. But the hardest truth—the one she could never say aloud—was this: he was probably the only soul alive who truly knew how losing Shane had shattered her.*

But Rainey wasn't sure what she was becoming. What she wanted.

She walked to the bed and sat slowly, the mattress creaking beneath her weight. She looked down at her hands. They had once been strong enough to pump Shane's chest with everything she had. But they had failed.

She had failed.

No matter how many people told her otherwise, no matter how many therapists used words like *trauma survivor* and *emotional resilience*, she still carried the truth like a scar inside her ribs.

She couldn't save the man she loved. She kept breathing, even when he stopped.

So what right did she have to want another?

Her eyes burned. She didn't cry.

There weren't many tears left.

Instead, she stood. Showered. Dressed in soft black jeans, a fitted sweater, and boots that made her stand an inch taller than she felt. She braided her hair loosely over one shoulder and applied a touch of mascara and some lip gloss. Not for anyone. Just to feel like she still existed. Like she *was*.

Her hands paused over the hotel room door.

Go out.

Just walk. Breathe. Move.

She grabbed her coat and stepped into the hall.

The hotel café was nearly empty.

Muted jazz played in the background. The clink of plates. The low murmur of voices. Rainey chose a corner booth near the window, ordered coffee and a slice of something sweet she wouldn't eat, and sat with her back to the wall.

She wasn't sure what she was looking for.

But she felt it again - that buzz under her skin. That pressure in the air.

A presence.

She looked up.

And there he was.

Jake.

Across the lobby. Standing near the concierge desk. Alone.

She froze.

He hadn't seen her yet. Or if he had, he gave no sign.

He wore a dark gray thermal shirt that clung to his chest and broad shoulders. Black jeans. Boots. A jacket slung casually over one arm. He wasn't talking to anyone-just...waiting.

He looked tired. Focused. Unreadable.

She couldn't breathe.

She didn't *want* to be seen.

And yet, if he walked away...

She wasn't sure she'd recover.

He turned.

His eyes met hers.

And the air between them *cracked.*

He didn't smile.

But he didn't look away either.

He walked toward her-not quickly, not slowly. Just... directly.

Each step landed like a drumbeat in her chest.

When he reached the table, he stopped. Didn't sit. Just stood there, looking at her like she was something rare.

"You're here," he said quietly.

"So are you," she replied.

"I wasn't sure I'd see you again."

She swallowed. "I….right."

He studied her face. Not in a rude way. Not invasive. Just… seeing.

"Can I sit?"

She nodded.

He slid into the booth across from her. His presence filled the space immediately. Like he expanded beyond his own body.

"I had a feeling I might run into you here," he said.

"You were looking for me?"

He didn't flinch. "I was hoping to find you."

Her stomach flipped.

"Why?"

Jake leaned forward slightly. "Because I don't usually notice people. But I noticed you. And I don't forget that kind of thing."

Her breath caught.

He wasn't flirting.

There was no charm. No line.

Just truth.

And it wrecked her.

She looked down at her coffee, hands trembling slightly. "I don't know how to do this."

"Do what?"

"This." She gestured at the space between them. "Connection. Trust. Idle chat."

His voice was low. "You don't have to know how. Just be honest. Be yourself."

"And if 'myself' is more turbulent than that flight?"

He smiled, "Then it's real."

Silence settled between them. Heavy. Not uncomfortable. But not light either.

He didn't ask for her number.

He didn't ask what room she was in.

He just sat with her. Solid. Present.

And it was *more* than she'd been given in years.

She reached for her coffee. Their fingers brushed.

And the ache returned - low and pulsing.

She wanted him.

But more than that, she wanted to be wanted. Deeply. Not as an escape. Not as a placeholder.

But as something *sacred*.

Her thighs pressed together beneath the table.

Jake's eyes dropped for half a second.

He saw.

She knew he saw.

She didn't adjust herself.

And he didn't look away.

Chapter Six

THE SURRENDER

Rainey

The second he touched her hand—even for a breath—her body betrayed her all over again.
It was nothing. Just a simple brush of skin. A fleeting warmth between fingertips over a mug of lukewarm coffee.

But it might as well have been a lightning strike—sharp, electric, unforgiving. It jolted something deep and dormant, something she'd sworn she'd buried with Shane. And in that instant, she hated how alive she suddenly felt.

Rainey curled her fingers around the coffee cup and tried to breathe normally. Jake's eyes hadn't moved from her face, but something between them had shifted – as if his stillness had a *direction* now. As if he'd decided what he wanted and she could feel it folding around her like a tide.

"Have you eaten?" he asked.

His voice was calm, measured. But beneath it, Rainey heard something harder. Not pressure. Just presence. A quiet expectation.

"No," she said. "I ordered something. I wasn't sure I'd actually…"

"Eat it?" he finished.

She nodded.

He leaned back slightly in the booth, his arms spreading casually along the top of the seat. "You need to."

"I struggle to keep things down."

He didn't blink. "You need to try."

The command wasn't loud. It wasn't harsh.

But it settled in her gut like gravity.

Something inside her – the part that had held herself together through two years of quiet collapse –*yielded*. Not in fear. Not out of weakness.

It felt like…relief.

She didn't have to think. She didn't have to decide. She just had to *listen*.

Rainey nodded slowly. "Okay."

His jaw flexed once. She caught it. So small. Most wouldn't have noticed.

But she did.

It was approval.

And God help her, it made her thighs ache.

The server returned with her pastry. She didn't remember ordering it, but now it sat in front of her: a delicate almond croissant, still warm.

Jake didn't touch the glass of bourbon he'd ordered.

He watched her instead.

Rainey tore a small piece and brought it to her mouth. She chewed slowly. Swallowed.

When she looked up, he hadn't moved.

"You're watching me eat?" she asked softly.

"I'm watching you submit to something more powerful than your resistance."

Her breath caught.

The word should've rattled her. *Submit.* It should've raised every feminist alarm bell in her brain. But instead… it wrapped around her spine and pulled tight.

She hadn't realized how badly she wanted someone to take over.

Just for a minute.

Just long enough to let her feel something besides grief and exhaustion.

Jake leaned forward slightly. "You're so tense. Not just emotionally. Your body's holding everything."

She froze.

"What makes you say that?"

He raised an eyebrow. "I've studied trauma. It doesn't just sit in your chest. It lives in your hips. Your shoulders. Your thighs."

Her pulse quickened.

"I've been trained to read people. You? You're clenched. Not because you're weak, but because you haven't let anyone help you carry the weight."

Rainey looked away.

"I'm impossible to ever fix," she whispered.

"I'm not trying to fix you."

She looked up again.

"I'm trying to see all the pieces of you and carry what's broken."

The words hit her like a blow. Not because they were dramatic – they weren't. They were true. Unadorned.

No man had ever spoken to her like that.
Not even Shane.

Shane had loved her with warmth and patience—tender, steady, sure. Their love had deepened over decades, unfolding like a slow bloom. But never, not even in the beginning, had he spoken with such raw possession… or looked at her like a man ready to burn the world down just to keep her.

Jake was different.

He didn't *ask* to protect her.
He claimed the role without hesitation, like it was already his.

And the worst part—the most terrifying, thrilling part—was that some hollow, starving part of her was already surrendering. Already reaching for the safety of his fire, even as it threatened to consume her.

The walk back to her room was a blur.

She didn't remember who stood first. She didn't remember what they said. Just his palm at the small of her back. Warm. Steady. Guiding.

It wasn't possessive.

It was commanding.

He didn't ask what floor she was on. He already knew. She didn't ask how. Maybe she'd told him. Maybe the desk had. She didn't care.

The elevator ride was silent.

But the tension? Loud.

Rainey couldn't look at him. If she did, she might fall apart. Or fall to her knees. She wasn't sure which.

She wanted him. Desperately. But it wasn't just lust. It was *need.* Raw and terrible.

She wanted his hands. His voice. His control. His consumption.

To give it *all* away. Just for a moment. Just to remember what it felt like to stop surviving and simply exist under someone else's will.

The elevator chimed. Her floor.

She stepped out. He followed.

Her keycard shook slightly as she held it to the door. The lock clicked open.

Inside, the room was still warm from her body.

She turned to him. Said nothing.

Jake stepped in behind her and closed the door.

And then silence.

He didn't pounce. He didn't speak.

He just looked at her.

Looked through her.

"Take off your coat," he said.

The tone was quiet. But it left no room for debate.

She complied.

Her fingers trembled as she slipped it from her shoulders and hung it over the chair.

She turned back to him, breath ragged.

Jake crossed the room slowly.

Not like a man in a hurry.

Like a man who had waited.

He stopped in front of her. Raised one hand. Touched the side of her face.

"I'm going to kiss you now" he said.

It sent chills all the way down her body.

His thumb brushed her lower lip. "Tell me you want this."

She didn't hesitate.

"I want this."

His mouth pressed to hers - not violently, not tenderly.

Completely.

The wettest, most passionate kiss she'd ever experienced. It was electric. Rainey melted.

His hands were everywhere - her jaw, her waist, her lower back, cascading down and all over, feeling her body withdraw and recoil briefly, only to lean into his every touch.

He didn't undress her. He didn't push for more.

He kissed her like a man claiming ground.

When he pulled back, she was shaking.

"You're okay," he said.

She nodded. Tears welled in her eyes. She didn't cry.

She just whispered: "Okay."

Jake kissed her forehead, then her temple.

Then he whispered, "Breathe for me."

And she did.

His lips were magic.

Not because they were soft – though they were. Not because he kissed her gently – he didn't. But because the second they touched hers, Rainey felt her soul *stop fighting*.

Jake's breath was warm on her mouth, and it sent shivers racing across her skin like a brushfire. He didn't rush. He didn't grope or press. He just *claimed* her lips – slowly, deeply, with devastating patience. His mouth moved over hers like he had all the time in the world.

And Rainey... she let him.

Her lips parted instinctively. A soft gasp slipped between them, and Jake inhaled it like a man tasting rain for the first time in years. His hand slid behind her neck, cradling it gently, thumb stroking the soft curve just beneath her ear.

She was trembling.

And he felt it. It invigorated him.

That's when the kiss changed.

What started as a delicate exploration turned into something hungrier. Jake pressed closer, deepening the kiss – not to dominate, but to possess. His other hand rested on her waist, firm and grounding.

Rainey moaned into his mouth, barely audible, but it lit him up like a fuse.

Jake's lips grew bolder. He tasted her fully, mouth opening against hers, tongue sweeping just once, testing, demanding. When she didn't pull away – when she *leaned in* – he pulled her tighter and kissed her again. Harder this time. Heavier. Deeper.

This wasn't supposed to happen.

It had been accidental, almost. Just a shared breath. Just a look. But the second his lips brushed hers, he hadn't been able to stop.

And when she didn't recoil – when she went soft in his arms and let him – something ancient and powerful surged inside him.

Control.

But not forced.

Granted.

He was used to women fighting for control. Used to games. Tests. Resistance.

But Rainey didn't resist.

She submitted to the kiss like her body had been waiting for it longer than she'd ever admit. And in that surrender, however small, Jake felt something he hadn't felt in years.

Empowered.

And not just in the sexual sense.

This was different.

Her compliance wasn't weak. It was STRENGTH.

It was *intentional.*

Her body spoke what her mouth didn't dare say:

"I want to be touched like this. I want to be taken."

And Jake heard her loud and clear.

When he finally broke the kiss, they were both breathing hard. Her face was flushed, her pupils wide, chest rising and falling beneath her sweater like a drum.

He didn't speak.

Neither did she.

Not right away.

Then, finally, Rainey whispered, "What… was that?"

Jake brushed his thumb across her cheekbone. "That was me not apologizing."

Her lips parted.

"For what?"

"For wanting you. For not letting fear or guilt stand between me and those beautiful lips."

Rainey closed her eyes.

And just like that, the dam cracked.

She wasn't afraid of him. That much was clear.

She was afraid of herself. Of what she'd just allowed. Of how it had made her feel – owned, seen, wanted in a way that wasn't just sweet and safe – but dangerous and raw.

Jake's voice dropped. "Open your eyes."

She did.

His gaze bore into hers. Not cruel. Not possessive.

Just certain.

"Did you want me to stop?"

She shook her head.

"Did you like the way my lips felt on your mouth? My hands on your body?"

A pause.

Then, with a shaky exhale: "Yes."

He nodded slowly, like her answers were permission granted.

"You're mine," he whispered, his voice low and rough against her skin. "Even if only for tonight."

The words weren't a claim. Not a command.
They were a confession.
A tremor of truth pulled from somewhere deep — where longing and fear lived side by side.

Rainey didn't flinch.
She didn't pull away.

She felt the heat of his breath at her neck, the weight of his need pressed into her like something sacred. Her fingers curled into his back, not to hold him down, but to hold herself steady.

Because she knew.
She was his.
In this hour. In this room.
In every part of herself that still remembered how to ache.

His hands moved slowly — reverent, unhurried — as if he knew she was something delicate and dangerous all at once. She gasped softly as his mouth brushed the curve of her shoulder, not from surprise, but from the overwhelming ache of being seen.

Not used.
Not claimed.
Chosen.

His touch wasn't just hunger — it was memory and mercy, grief and gratitude, poured into every inch of her skin.

She let herself fall into him, not because she was weak — but because something in him had finally matched the quiet storm inside her.

And in that dim, breathless space between them, where time felt suspended and the world fell silent, they found something neither of them had dared to ask for:

Not possession.
Not escape.

But the brief, holy illusion of belonging.

Even if only for tonight.

Chapter Seven

THE LINGERING

Jake

Jake hadn't slept.
Not a minute.

He lay still on that stiff, unfamiliar mattress, the ceiling above him fading in and out of focus. His eyes were open, but he wasn't seeing. Not really. His body was still, but inside, he was a live wire—every nerve lit up and fraying.

Not because of danger.
Not because of work.
Because of her.

Rainey.

Every time he blinked, she was there.

Not just a memory, but a presence. A weight on his chest. A ghost wrapped in silk and sorrow and something that tasted like salvation.

Her face — God, that face — etched into his mind like a scar he didn't want to heal. The soft lines of her mouth, the way her lashes swept down just before he kissed her... it haunted him.

But it wasn't the kiss that broke him.

It was her eyes.

Not afraid. Not shy. They'd looked at him like they already knew who he was beneath the surface. Like they recognized every part of him—flaws and shadows included—and didn't look away.

She had met him in that kiss. Matched him. And then surrendered.

That kind of thing? You don't fake it. You don't teach it. You either have it… or you don't.

And *she* had it.

It lit him on fire.

His chest rose and fell in shallow bursts, the air too tight in his lungs. His jaw ached from the tension. His fists curled and uncurled on the sheets, still imagining the feel of her waist beneath his palms. The slight tremble in her breath when he leaned in. The helpless sound she made when his tongue teased the edge of her lips.

Jesus.

He hadn't even touched her skin. Hadn't seen her bare. Hadn't pressed her into the mattress or pulled her hips to his.

But it didn't matter.

That kiss?

It was *possession*.

It was a promise.

And it had ruined him.

Jake had kissed women before. Hundreds. Maybe more.
He wasn't proud of the number.
But it was the truth.

He had lived fast. Moved faster. Worked in shadows, slipped in and out of hotel rooms and war zones with the same detachment. Women came and went like warm weather. Some sweet. Some wild. Some forgettable before dawn.

And he'd been fine with that.

He liked solitude. It was safe. Predictable.

But this?
This wasn't sex.
This wasn't release or routine.

This was a damn revelation.

A kiss that didn't end when it ended — it stayed behind, clawing at the back of his throat, burning down his spine.

Rainey had opened for him. Mouth soft, body still, hands unsure… but her soul had surged forward. And he'd felt it.

Every inch of her need.

Every ounce of her ache.

And she had let him take it.

He hadn't asked.
He hadn't needed to.
He just knew.

Because it was in the way her breath caught. The way her knees didn't buckle, but her lips did. The way her mouth had molded perfectly against his like it belonged there.

And maybe it did.

God help him.

Because the more he replayed it, the more he realized — he didn't want anyone else ever knowing what that felt like.

He sat up slowly, raking a hand through his hair, the bedsheet tangled low across his hips. His room was dim, bathed in early morning light. Outside, the city was beginning to stir. A horn honked in the distance. Someone slammed a car door. A siren echoed far off.

But inside, everything was still.

Except for him.

Jake stood, bare feet hitting the cold floor. He stretched his shoulders, the muscles in his back tight from a night spent holding tension like a weapon. He moved to the window and stared out into the fog-laced skyline.

He didn't smoke.
But God, he wanted to.

Something to burn. Something to calm the thing crawling through his veins.

Because she was still there — not just in his head, but under his skin.

He wondered if she'd slept.

If her mouth still tasted like him. If her lips were still swollen from their kiss. If her heart was still racing from what he'd whispered against her throat just before he pulled back.

"You're mine. Even if only for tonight."

He hadn't meant to say it.

It had just… spilled out. Unfiltered. Raw.

Because it was true.

He hadn't claimed her body. But he had claimed something else. Something deeper.

He wanted her.

Not for a night.
Not for a fix.
He wanted to *belong* to her.

And that was the part that scared him most.

Jake wasn't built for this.

He was forged in fire. Trained to compartmentalize. To react, to survive, to endure.

He'd buried people. Seen things that fractured lesser men. He'd carried children out of rubble. Held dying men in his arms. Made decisions that would follow him to the grave.

And through it all, he had stayed in control.

Until now.

Because Rainey hadn't come at him with fire.

She came with silence. With softness. With a stillness that undid him.

And that terrified him.

Because he recognized it.

He knew what it was to carry grief like a backpack full of bricks. To keep going because stopping would mean collapse. To show up, protect others, and fall apart in private.

And Rainey?

She carried that grief with grace.

She didn't ask him for anything. Didn't try to fill his silence with words.

She just… *saw him.*

And he saw her.

And now, the thought of another man seeing her that way— touching her, holding her, kissing that mouth that had opened for him like a gift?

He wanted to tear the goddamn world apart.

He went to the hotel gym to burn it off.

Ran until his legs trembled.

Boxed the heavy bag until his knuckles split and the leather stung like truth.

It didn't help.

Every breath hurt. Every punch landed with her name behind it.

When the sweat soaked through his shirt and the pounding in his ears drowned out the noise in his head, he finally stopped.

Showered.

Let the scalding water hit his back like a punishment.

He closed his eyes and leaned forward against the tile, forehead resting on cool porcelain, water running down his face like confession.

He heard her voice.

"I want this."

It was quiet. Frightened. Brave.

It was the kind of want you confess only when your whole soul is starving.

And she'd given it to him.

Trusted him with it.

God help the man who ever took that trust and crushed it.

Jake gritted his teeth and turned off the water.

His hands shook as he dried off and pulled on clean clothes. His body still hummed with need, his chest tight with something unspoken.

By the time he stepped into the hallway, a decision had taken root in his gut like steel.

He had to see her again.

To hear her voice.

To look into her eyes and know—not wonder—whether she felt it too.
This pull. This obsession.
This thing that had wrapped around his ribs like a vice and whispered:

"She's yours.
And if you lose her…
you won't survive it."

Chapter Eight

THE LONGING

Rainey

She hadn't stopped shaking.

Not visibly. No one would have known. But under her skin, just beneath the surface, her nerves hummed with something between electricity and grief. Like her body hadn't decided whether to fall apart or burst open.

Rainey sat at the edge of the bed in her hotel room, the morning light filtering through heavy curtains. Her phone lay untouched beside her. Coffee gone cold. She stared at her knees, hands folded tightly in her lap like she was bracing for impact.

What did you do?

She had kissed a stranger.

No.....she had let a stranger kiss her. Not a gentle, curious brush of lips. Not a timid test.

She had *surrendered* her mouth to him.

And he had taken it like it already belonged to him.

Jake.

Even his name made her chest ache.

She hadn't expected to feel this way. She hadn't expected to feel *anything*. She had come here only to escape the vacuum of her life.

Not to step into a new one. Not to collapse into someone else's arms, someone else's control, someone else's heat.

But God... his mouth.

His mouth had been soft and firm and sure. His breath had tickled her lips before he ever touched them, and when he finally did-when he pulled her into him with a quiet, terrifying certainty-something in her body had roared awake. Something *explosive*.

She hadn't known she could feel like that.

Not anymore.

Not after Shane.

Not after the screams, the sirens, the sound of her son's voice breaking in real time.

She should be ashamed. She should be terrified.

Instead, she felt like she was rising. Slowly. Painfully. From the cold ground she had been living on for almost two years.

Jake didn't smile much. He didn't flirt. But he saw her. Really *saw* her.

And more than that...he shared something with her.

Pain.

It was there in his eyes, buried under the steel. Something old. Something that hadn't healed right. He had been abandoned. Burned. Discarded. And instead of growing bitter, he had grown dangerous.

But not in a way that scared her.

In a way that made her feel *safe*.

Because she knew-the second his lips pressed to hers – that if she gave herself to him, *he wouldn't drop her.*

He wouldn't walk away and forget.

He would keep her.

And the idea of belonging to someone like that... someone who wouldn't break her out of carelessness or cowardice...

It didn't feel degrading.

It felt like air.

You're mine, he'd said.

At least for now.

And that's when it hit her-the weight of how badly she needed this to be real.

Not because she was desperate. But because it was her only chance to rise from the abyss.

Since Shane died, her life felt like shattered glass — cold, fragile, and a broken transparence the rest of the world pitied but wanted to avoid.

She moved through the days like a shadow of herself – almost catatonic in her own shallow existence; setting her alarm to wake Dillon for school, preparing meals, folding laundry, and performing the mundane motions of a life that no longer felt like her own.

And inside?
Inside, she was in ruin. Who *was* she?
The woman she'd been had crumbled the moment Shane's heart stopped, and what remained was a ravaged shell — quiet, empty. Even as she wailed, she was completely numb.

And if it weren't for Dillon…God only knows.
If not for HIM.

The weight of his arms around her neck or the sound of his voice anchoring her to this world —
She wouldn't survive it.
She wouldn't want to.

It was that brutal.
That honest.
That *unbearably* real.

But Jake…

Jake sparked something inside of her that made her feel like she *existed* again.

Not as a mother.

Not as a widow.

As *Rainey*.

As a *woman*.

She rose slowly and crossed to the mirror, bracing herself against the truth staring back.
Same long blonde hair, pulled into a loose braid. Same bare face, unpainted and clean. Her sweater still slipped carelessly off one shoulder, exposing skin she hadn't bothered to notice in years.
But tonight—God, tonight—she *felt* different.

There was something new in her eyes.
Something raw.
Something *undeniably* alive.

She looked beautiful. Not in the way Shane used to call her pretty on Sunday mornings. Not in the way strangers complimented her grace or poise.

This was different.
This was *a wanting*.

She looked like a woman on the edge of being *resurrected*. And for the first time, she didn't feel ashamed of it. She felt *powerful*.

She thought of his hands—large, rough, certain. The way they'd deliberately settled on her body like they'd been searching for her all along.

She thought of his voice, low and gravel-edged, curling around her name like a promise and a threat.
And then... she thought of his pain. How it clung to him like armor, heavy and unspoken.

She had seen it—felt it—before he ever admitted it.
Because something in him was broken.
And it looked just like the wound inside her.

Maybe that was what pulled her in more than anything else. Not just the hunger. Not just the heat.
But the *ache* she recognized as her own.

She knew what it would mean to let him in—all the way in.
It wouldn't be safe.
He could ruin her. Strip her down to nothing.
But walking away now?

That might be worse.
Because for the first time in years, she wasn't just surviving.
She was *burning.*
And she wasn't ready to go cold again.

Jake

He stood just outside the hotel café again, pretending to read the news on his phone.

She hadn't come down.

He'd waited nearly an hour.

Jake wasn't a man who lingered. He didn't chase. He didn't show his hand.

But *this* woman had ruined that.

He'd barely slept. Barely eaten. He'd trained himself not to feel hunger – emotional or physical –unless it served a purpose.

But this wasn't hunger.

This was **need**.

Rainey wasn't just a woman.

She was oxygen.

Warmth.

A chance to belong to something that *mattered.*

He kept seeing her eyes. The way they'd widened when he told her to take off her coat. Not afraid. Ready. Like her whole body had been waiting for someone to notice she was still alive.

And that kiss…
It hadn't just stirred something.
It had *rearranged* him.

Something in him shifted the moment her mouth met his. Like a fuse was lit in a place he didn't know existed—slow, dangerous, inevitable.
Now, he couldn't stop. Couldn't breathe without thinking about her. How she'd taste when he took his time.
How her voice would sound, breathless and trembling, whispering his name into the dark.
How she'd look on her knees—not because he demanded it, but because she *chose* it.

Not for sex.
Not for pleasure.
But for surrender.

That's what haunted him most.
She hadn't just melted under his touch—she'd yielded. Completely. Instinctively.

And Jake had never known that kind of surrender. Not real. Not raw. Not without strings or masks or performance.
But with Rainey, it had been *pure.*
Undeniable.

And now, it was *in him.* Like blood. Like fire.

He needed to see her again.
Even if it was just once.
Even if it ended in silence and regret.
He needed her to know—this wasn't casual. Not for him. Not even close.

His phone was in his hand before he could talk himself out of it.
His thumb hovered over the search bar—her hotel, the one he swore he wouldn't check.
But he did.

Because if he waited too long...
If he let fear or logic win...

He'd lose her.
And this time, the hollow left behind might just *finish* him.

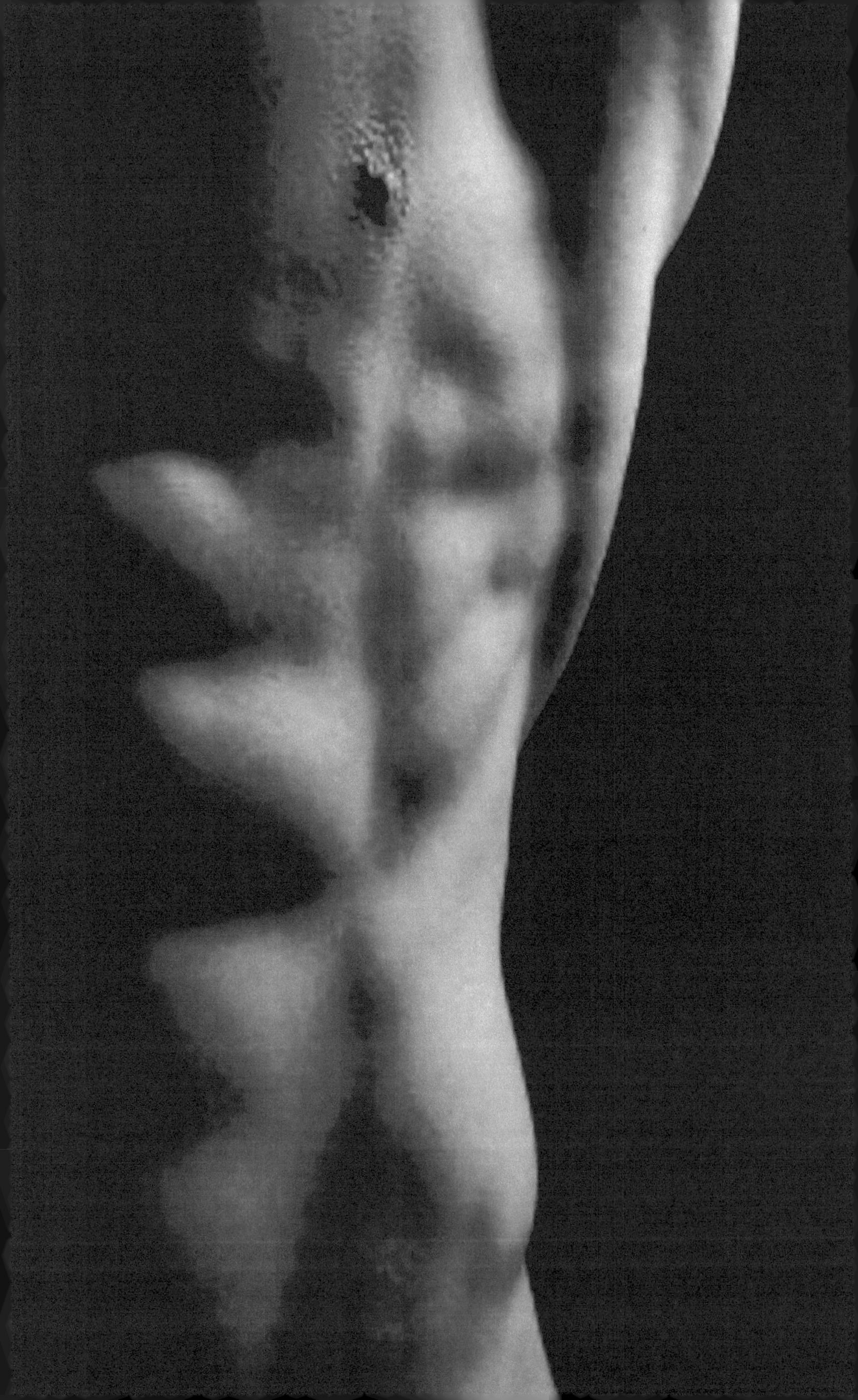

Chapter Nine

THE YEARNING

Rainey

The knock was soft.

So soft, she almost convinced herself she'd imagined it.

But then it came again - a firm, measured sound. Like whoever stood on the other side of the door already knew she'd answer. Not "if," but "when."

Her breath caught in her throat.

She stood frozen near the foot of the bed, heart pounding, palms damp. Part of her wanted to run. The other part - the darker, needier part - already knew who it was.

Jake.

God.

Her hand trembled as she reached for the doorknob.

She hesitated.

Was she ready?

No.

Was she willing?

Yes.

She turned the handle.

And there he was.

He stood in the doorway—tall, broad, cut from shadow and light. The hallway glow poured over his shoulders like liquid gold, tracing the hard lines of muscle beneath his shirt, the tension in his stance, the coiled restraint in his frame.

A virtual wall of strength and silence.

His face partially camouflaged in shadow, unreadable—but his presence hit first. Heavy. Commanding. Magnetic. The kind of energy that changed the air, slowed time. A gravitational force that caused everything else to fall away.

Every inch of him radiated heat and danger, the quiet kind that didn't have to speak to be obeyed.
And still, it was the way he looked at her that unraveled her completely—like she was his to take, his to ruin, his to worship.

She couldn't move.
Didn't want to.
Not with that kind of power standing there... waiting.

There was something feral in the way he looked at her. Not lust alone—*possession*.
Like she was the only thing tethering him to the earth.
Like nothing else existed. Nothing else *mattered*.

And God help her... she didn't want to be anywhere else but under that gaze.

And then his eyes softened. Just slightly.

"May I come in?" he asked, voice low.

Rainey nodded.

He stepped inside, quiet as a shadow, and gently closed the door behind him.

Neither of them moved.

The air between them hummed-a silent, dangerous promise.

Jake's gaze moved slowly over her body, not in lust, but in *claiming*. As if reminding himself she was real.

She turned slightly, fingers brushing the lamp on the nightstand.

Jake's voice stopped her.

"Leave it on."

She paused, hand hovering.

"I want to see you," he added gently.

Heat bloomed up her neck.

She lowered her hand and turned back to him.

Jake took two steps closer.

Still no rush. Just gravity.

Then he reached out and touched her jaw, fingers warm, careful.

"I want to take off your clothes," he said.
The words weren't crude. They were reverent. Anchored in restraint.
Still, Rainey stood frozen — her breath shallow, trapped somewhere between her ribs and her throat.

Jake stepped closer, the heat of his body wrapping around her like a current.
"I want you to let me," he said again, voice lower now, more certain.
A whisper edged with hunger.

She didn't speak.
She couldn't.
Her mouth parted, her heart thundering like it might break free of her chest.

He reached for her, one hand resting at her waist, the other lifting her chin gently until her eyes met his. "Tell me yes."

The word caught at the edge of her lips.
A beat. A breath.
And then, almost too soft to be real:
"Yes."

Only then did his hands move — slow, intentional. His fingers found the hem of her sweater and paused there, brushing lightly over the fabric as if asking one last time.

Then he lifted it, inch by inch, his thumbs gliding over the sensitive skin of her ribs, her sides.
She gasped — not from surprise, but from the intimacy of it.
From the way he watched her.

Not for permission anymore.
But for the moment she let go.

When her sweater hit the floor, he stepped back to take her in.
His gaze traveled over her body, lingering on the curves of her breasts, the soft line of her belly, the quick rise and fall of her breath.
But he didn't touch.
Not yet.

He looked at her like she was something rare — something he'd waited for.
And Rainey, bare from the waist up, felt the heat crawl up her neck, flush through her chest.
She had never felt more exposed.
Or more seen.

Jake circled her slowly, stepping behind her.
His fingers slid into her braid and began to undo it, gently loosening strand after strand until her hair fell free across her back in soft waves.
He came back around to face her. Brushed a single lock of hair from her lips with the back of his knuckles.

Then, without a word, he unhooked her bra.
It slid down her arms like a whisper. He caught it before it fell.
And when she stood before him — bare, trembling, waiting — he didn't pounce.

He worshipped.

He reached up, fingertips grazing her collarbone, trailing slowly to the curve of her shoulder.
"Beautiful," he said, like it was fact. Like it was the only word that existed.

His mouth followed — warm, slow, and purposeful.
He kissed her neck. Her shoulder. The hollow below her ear.
Every press of his lips ignited something low and steady inside her.

Then his hands moved to her waist.
"Lie down," he said, nodding to the couch by the window.

She obeyed.
Not out of submission.
But trust.

The cushions were cool beneath her back. Her legs bent at the knees, still clothed in her leggings and the thin lace of her panties.
Jake knelt beside her.
The muscles in his arms tensed as he braced himself, hovering over her.
His eyes had darkened — not with lust alone, but reverence. Focus. Intention.

"I want your thighs open," he said, his hand settling on the tender inside of her leg.

The words were barely a whisper, but they rippled through her — heat and tension blooming in their wake.

Her breath caught — but her legs moved.
She opened for him.

His hands landed on her knees, firm but patient, and slowly slid downward — his palms brushing her skin, fingertips grazing the outer seams of her leggings. He gave a gentle pull.
Her thighs parted farther.

He said nothing.
But his eyes did.
She saw the shift in him — the way his chest rose slightly, the quiet sound that escaped his lips.
Approval.
Desire.
Awe.

He leaned down, his mouth a breath above her navel, and kissed her belly — slow, reverent. Then lower. And lower still.
Her body tightened beneath him, a soft sound escaping her lips.

He took his time peeling off her leggings, inch by careful inch, until they were gone.
Her panties remained.
Sheer. Damp. Vulnerable.

He didn't remove them.
Not yet.

His thumbs stroked along the lace edge, where skin met fabric. The most sensitive place.
Then he looked up at her, eyes sharp and hungry — but gentle.
"I'm going to take these off," he said, "but not until you want me to."

She tried drawing a sharp breath, but a good shiver stole her inhale.
She had never been asked that before.
Never been touched like this — with such patience. Such command wrapped in care.

"I want you to," she whispered.

Jake slid his fingers beneath the waistband and drew them down — slowly, unbearably slow — like he was uncovering a secret. Like this was not lust, but reverence.
He watched her the whole time.
Watched the rise of her chest. The tremble in her thighs. The soft part of her lips.
When the fabric fell away, he didn't dive between her legs.

He paused.
Looked.

Admired.

He kissed the inside of her thighs. Then higher. Then stopped.

"I love your body," he murmured.
The words weren't rehearsed. They were raw.

Rainey's heart stopped.
And then stuttered back to life.

Jake leaned in and kissed her — long, aching, and slow — the kind of kiss that didn't ask for anything but gave everything.
His mouth trailed to her arm, to the faint scar that lived there — a forgotten wound only she still thought about.
He kissed it. Slowly.

Then, with devastating tenderness, he laid his hand over her heart. "Perfection," he whispered, voice hoarse. "Even your scars… especially your scars. Absolute perfection."

Chapter Ten

THE RUINS

Rainey

She could still feel his breath between her thighs long after he'd kissed his way back up her body.

He hadn't taken her. Hadn't even touched her where she ached the most. But her body pulsed like he had — as if every nerve had been lit with careful intention and left there to smolder.

She was bare now — naked on the couch, her thighs still parted, her skin flushed and tender, the cool air prickling over places that had never felt so exposed. The soft amber glow from the lamp cast a halo across her hips, catching the sheen of moisture that clung to her.

Her breath came in shallow pulls. Each one a reminder.

She was no longer a woman untouched by want.

She was opened. Not by penetration — not yet — but by the weight of his mouth on her skin and the words he hadn't yet spoken.

Jake knelt beside her, half-shadowed by the lamplight. One knee on the rug, the other foot flat on the ground. Poised. Balanced. Controlled.

His expression was unreadable. But his silence? That vibrated louder than anything. Like a storm held back by sheer will.

He watched her.

Not like a man with permission.

But like one who had just witnessed something sacred — and was deciding whether he could survive stepping any further inside.

She swallowed hard. Her lips parted, but she didn't know what to say. Then, almost without thinking, she whispered:

"I need to touch you."

The words startled her. They rose from the same dark, hungry place that made her say *yes* when he told her to lie back… the place that didn't want gentleness, not now — the place that wanted to be claimed.

Jake's breath caught. His head tilted slightly, like he was studying something rare.

He didn't speak right away.

Instead, he sat back on his heels and let the moment hang between them. The room stilled. Her heartbeat thundered in her ears.

Then, finally, his voice came — low, steady, laced with something primal.

"Stand up."

Her knees shook as she obeyed. She rose slowly, her body trembling with more than arousal — it was reverence, fear, anticipation, and the sharp edge of emotional exposure.

Jake rose with her.

And then she was reminded just how much larger he was. His full height eclipsed her. His body — broad, cut, grounded — made her feel small in a way that was strangely comforting.

She tilted her chin to meet his eyes.

He didn't move.

Didn't touch her.

But she felt the pull between them like a tether — something invisible but unbreakable.

His jaw flexed once. His eyes softened, then darkened again.

"You're sacred in every way," he said.

The words stunned her. They hit like a benediction.

Her breath caught. Her throat tightened. She opened her mouth, but whatever response she had vanished under the weight of his gaze.

Then, Jake reached for her hand. Slowly. Deliberately. He guided it to the hem of his shirt.

"You want to touch me?" he asked, voice barely above a whisper. "Start here."

Her hands moved before her mind could stop them. She gripped the edge of his shirt and began to lift. The cotton slid up over ridged muscle, over his abdomen, over a body that looked carved from hardship and war.

He was beautiful.

But not like men in magazines — not sculpted for vanity.

He was *solid.*

Every line of him told a story. Old bruises. Faint scars. Strength earned, not given.

Her fingers traced one jagged scar along his rib. She paused there.

She didn't ask.

He didn't offer.

But his gaze stayed locked with hers.

Unflinching.

She continued, her hands reverent now. She didn't just want to *see* him. She wanted to *know* him — through touch, through skin, through memory.

At his belt, her fingers slowed.

Jake's breath deepened. "Keep going."

So she did.

The belt. The button. The zipper. Each one louder than it should have been, amplified by the silence between them. Her fingers trembled, but not from hesitation — from awe.

He was already hard.

Thick and urgent beneath his boxer briefs.

She didn't look up. She didn't speak. She just pulled the waistband down, exposing him fully.

And then she froze.

He was… **magnificent**.

Large. Heavy. Veined. Hard in a way that made her breath catch and her thighs clench without meaning to.

But what stunned her most was the way he stood — still, hands at his sides, giving her space to look. To choose.

He made no move to cover himself.

He wasn't cocky. He wasn't teasing.

He was giving her a kind of honor — letting her see him like this. Letting her decide what came next.

Then, he stepped forward just enough to cradle her face.

"Touch me."

It wasn't a suggestion.

It wasn't even a plea.

It was a **command** — velvet-wrapped and thick with restraint.

Her hand moved to him. Then her mouth. She wrapped her lips around him, careful, gentle.

The sound he made — low, guttural — ripped through her. His head tilted back slightly, a muscle in his neck twitching as she began to glide back and forth, gently licking and moving her tongue.

Slow at first.

Learning him.

Memorizing him.

The shape. The texture. The weight of him.

Her fingers caressing. Her thumb grazed the head. He growled, deep and low.

His hands wrapped around the curls that cascaded down her delicate back, not pulling, just holding — grounding them both.

He let her lead. But she could feel the control vibrating through him.

He was letting her consume him.

But only just.

Then, without warning, he caught her wrist.

Not rough. Not reprimanding.

Just redirecting.

He guided her upward, placed her hand firmly over his chest.

His heart was thundering beneath her bottom lip.

"Not tonight," he said.

She blinked. Her pulse stuttered. Heat rushed up her throat.

"I don't want to lose control."

Her voice broke. "You think I want control?"

That made him smile.

A slow, dangerous smile that made her knees wobble.

"No," he said.
"I think you want to surrender."

His mouth brushed her collarbone.

Her neck.

The tender space just beneath her jaw.

His lips barely moved as he whispered:

"And I want to earn you. Savor you."

She shivered violently.

Not from cold.
From everything.

Jake leaned closer, his breath hot against her ear.

"When I take you, Rainey," he murmured,
"you'll be begging for it. And I won't stop until you forget every name but mine."

The sound that escaped her lips wasn't voluntary. A gasp. A moan. Something *raw*.

He pulled back to see her face.

The wide eyes. The parted lips.

Then he kissed her — **hard**.

No prelude. No hesitation. Just hunger. Just possession.

And when he pulled away, his voice was steel. "Put your clothes on."

She didn't move.

So he kissed her again – Short. Firm. Final.

Then stepped back.

"Now."

The command hit her like a spark to dry leaves.

Not fear. Not shame.

But something darker. Something thrilling.
Something that made her feel alive in a way she hadn't in years.

She moved slowly.

Panties first. Then her sweater.

The fabric scraped over overstimulated skin.

She could still feel his breath.

His mouth.

Him.

Jake dressed with the same calm precision he brought to everything — each motion efficient, intentional.

By the time she turned to face him again, he stood with one hand braced on the wall, breathing like a man who'd just stepped away from a fire and left part of himself in the flames.

His eyes found hers.

"I want to see you again tomorrow."

His voice was rough.

"Dinner."

She nodded.

He stepped closer.

"That's a yes, right beautiful?"

Her throat tightened. But she managed it.

"Yes."

He cupped her face, his thumb brushing her cheek with reverence.

"That's my good girl."

Then he kissed her forehead.

Turned.

And left.

The door didn't slam.
It clicked softly shut.

But the silence he left behind roared in her ears.

She was dressed now.

But still bare.

Still trembling.

Still undone.

Chapter Eleven
RESISTANCE

Jake

He walked away like he still had control.

But he didn't.

Not really.

His jaw clenched so tight his teeth ached. His hands were fists. His back was slick with sweat under his shirt, even though the hallway was cool and still.

He hadn't looked back when he left her room.

If he had, he wouldn't have left at all.

Jake made it to the elevator and hit the button with too much force. It lit immediately, but he didn't move. He stared at the silver doors like they were holding him back from going to war.

Because it *felt* like war.

Like he'd walked off a battlefield where every instinct screamed: *Stay. Take her. Mark her.*

And he hadn't.

He'd walked away.

Because if he hadn't…

He would've taken too much.

She was already shaking when he kissed her thighs. Already gasping when he told her she was his.

Another five seconds and she would've let him do anything.

And that terrified him.

Not because she was weak — she wasn't.

Because she was willing.

And he didn't know how to be careful with something that surrendered to him so completely.

That kind of trust? That kind of vulnerability?

He didn't deserve it.

I want you to let me.

He'd said those words out loud. Given her the chance to say no.

But when she didn't answer, when she stood frozen and trembling with her mouth parted and her chest rising and falling, it had flipped something inside him.

Tell me yes.

And she had.

He could still hear it.

Still feel it echo in his chest like it had hit some hidden, hungry part of his soul that had been starving for years.

And then she'd touched him — soft, reverent, like *he* was the fragile one. He'd barely held it together when her fingers wrapped around him.

Not tonight, he told her.

Because if he hadn't stopped her, he would've come undone. Right there. In her mouth. And something about that — about being that *exposed* in front of someone who mattered — was too much.

He wasn't ready.

Not yet.

Because now that he had her in his hands — now that her body was starting to open for him, her walls crumbling, her voice whispering yes — he knew one thing with terrifying clarity:

If he lost her, he wouldn't come back from it.

Rainey

Rainey lay on her side in the dark, the sheets twisted around her legs, Jake's scent still clinging to her skin. Sleep refused to come. Her body throbbed with the aftershocks of touch withheld, of a fire lit but not consumed. But it wasn't just her body that kept her awake. It started with the feel of breath on her skin—Jake's breath—still ghosting between her thighs like a wave crashing and retreating, leaving her bare and aching like sand pulled from underfoot.

The Alabama Gulf coastline.
That beautiful utopia where everything once came together for them as a family. Where they built their business and their first home. Where they saved for years—thousands—for IVF treatments. And where Dillon was born.

When everything was whole.
Before it all slipped away.

It was spring—soft and fragrant—the kind of warm that clung to your skin and slowed time. They weren't married yet. Just two people in love, still learning each other's edges. He had taken her halfway across the country to meet his parents, and they'd gone to dinner at The Grand—a waterfront hotel, golf course and restaurant in Fairhope, lush with trees that scraped the sky and sweeping views of Mobile Bay.

Afterward, they walked the grounds—her heels in one hand, his jacket slung over his shoulder. The sun was dipping low, casting gold across the manicured lawn. That's when she saw it.

A magnolia tree.
Just like the one that stood in her yard when she was a little girl in Louisiana.

Towering. Elegant. In full bloom.
Its branches stretched wide like arms open in welcome, blossoms heavy with scent and softness. She paused to admire it—said something offhand about how beautiful it was, how regal.

And without a word, Shane looked up, smiled, and climbed the damn thing.
In his suit.

He scrambled up like a boy with scraped knees and no fear of falling. She laughed—shocked, delighted—and tried to stop him, but he only waved her off. Moments later, he came down with a single blossom, pristine and perfect, cradled in his hand like something sacred.

He ran to her, tie crooked, hair mussed, and pressed the flower into her palm.
Then he kissed her cheek—lips warm and sure—and whispered,
"You're the most beautiful thing I've ever seen."

Even now, she could feel that moment in her bones.
The weight of the flower.
The smell of magnolia.
The quiet certainty in his voice.

She wondered now if she'd truly appreciated it then—how many small, extraordinary things like that he would do.
Not grand gestures.
Not headlines.
Just a hundred quiet offerings of love.

And now, with silence all around her and memory tightening in her chest, she ached at the thought:
Those moments weren't small at all.
They were emblematic and everlasting.

She lay still in the hotel bed, her body clothed but not covered, the sheets pushed aside, her skin bare to the cool air, her thighs still tingling where his hands had been. Her sweater was rumpled, underwear back in place, but her body hadn't caught up to the idea that it was over—whatever *it* had been. Not yet. Maybe not ever.

Her mind spun, cluttered with that cruel mix of chaos and desire.

Jake was gone.
But everything he'd done still lingered.

His mouth.
His breath.
His voice in her ear.
His hands on her thighs—firm, reverent, claiming.

And the command.
God, the command.

She had never been told what to do like that—not gently, not
with such quiet authority. Not by someone who didn't want to
overpower her, but to hold her steady. To make her feel safe in
surrender.

Jake hadn't manhandled her. He hadn't needed to.
He had guided her with a calm certainty that had bypassed her
mind and gone straight to her marrow. Like he *knew*. Knew what
she needed. Knew the ache she'd kept buried so long she almost
forgot it had teeth.

And she had obeyed.
Willingly.

It should have scared her.
But what terrified her more was how much she'd *loved* it.

She closed her eyes, desperate to shut off her brain. But all she saw
was him—kneeling beside her, jaw clenched, eyes locked on hers
as he pulled her thighs apart like she was something sacred. Telling
her what he wanted like he'd waited years to say it.

And what shattered her now... was how badly she had *wanted* to
give it to him.

God.
What was she doing?

She had a son.
She was a *widow*.
She had spent nearly two years walking through life as a half-
person. Mothering. Managing. Surviving. But not living. Not
wanting.

And now here she was — aching for a man she barely knew. A man who kissed her once and made her feel more *real* than she had in years.

And that was the part that wrecked her.
Not the heat.
Not the hunger.
The *realness*.

It wasn't sex. It wasn't even lust.
It was that, in the moment she looked into his eyes, she stopped feeling like a ghost.

And now... she was terrified.

Because if he disappeared—
If he decided this was too much, or not enough—
If he saw the jagged pieces she still carried and decided he didn't want to touch them—

She didn't know if she could survive that.
Not again.

She rolled onto her back and stared at the ceiling, trying to breathe through the rising panic. She swallowed hard, sat up slowly, and glanced at the clock.

Dinner.
He was expecting her.
Expecting *more* from her.

And for the first time in years, she *wanted* to give it.
Not to prove anything.
Not to replace what she'd lost.

But because something inside her was waking up again.
And Jake—this quiet, guarded man—had sparked the match.

She placed her bare feet on the floor, her skin still tingling, her body still open.
And she whispered aloud into the empty room, as if confessing to herself,
"Please... don't disappear."

Then she rose.
And began to get ready.

Chapter Twelve

SUBMERSION

Rainey

Dinner had been warm and unpretentious — a quaint Italian bistro tucked on a quiet corner with candlelit tables and soft jazz playing through old speakers. The conversation flowed effortlessly, even as they navigated the heavy, intimate corners of their lives — revealing pieces of themselves that mattered most, without ever needing to force the words. He let her order first. Shared his wine without asking. Made her laugh more than she expected. There was a moment when he reached across the table to wipe a dot of sauce from the corner of her mouth, and her breathing fractured for a beat. Not because it was forward. But because it was so simple, so intimate. Like they'd done this a dozen times before. Like it wasn't new. Like it was natural.

As they stepped off the curb and into the soft glow of the parking lot, he slipped his jacket over her shoulders and pulled her gently to his side, his hand settling at her waist — protective, certain. The night air wrapped around them, cool and quiet, but it was the silence between them that felt warmest. It wasn't awkward. It wasn't empty. It was full — of shared laughter, unspoken truths, and something tender growing in the spaces between their words. Neither of them spoke a word. The entirety of that moment spoke for itself.

He opened the door for her — not performative, not casual. Just steady. Expectant. Like she was something valuable being moved from one place to another. Not breakable. Not fragile. But precious. Strong.

Inside was quiet. Dark leather. Dim dashboard lights. Impeccably clean. The engine purred beneath her feet, low and smooth like everything else about him. He reached down and put on a pair of black-framed Oakley prescription glasses. They matured him in a surprisingly pleasing way. He made a passing comment about "needing them."

She liked that. More than she could explain. Maybe because it made him human. Maybe because it reminded her that even men like him needed help to see clearly.

He didn't turn on the music. Just drove, immersing himself in the rhythm of everything Rainey.

His right hand moved from the gear shift to her thigh — not in a casual, flirty way, but possessive. Commanding. He glanced over and looked into her eyes.

Her dress had ridden up slightly as she sat. His fingers rested there now, on the bare skin above her knee. He didn't move them. Didn't stroke or grip. He didn't need to.

She felt his pulse through his fingertips.

And she kept her legs still. Just as he'd left them.

Jake fixed his eyes ahead on the road again, but his hand squeezed once.

"Good girl," he murmured.

A pulse rippled through her chest — warm, bright, and terrifying. She didn't know she needed to hear that. But now she never wanted to go without it again.

She clenched her thighs. Testing. Jake squeezed again. "Don't."

She turned to look at him, eyes wide.

He gave the faintest shake of his head. "You keep those legs exactly where they are."

She flushed hot all over. "Yes," she whispered.

"Say it louder."

"Yes, Jake."

His thumb traced one slow, lazy circle on her thigh. "Beautiful...and obedient."

His home was impressive. Much larger than she expected and definitely more space than he needed. But it was clean. Masculine. Quiet. Almost a reflection of him.

Dark wood floors. Heavy furniture.

Not impersonal, but lonely. No clutter. No softness. Just space and strength.

He opened the door and let her in first.

She stepped inside and looked around. The air smelled like cedar and soap. Like him.

Jake followed, slowly shutting the door behind them. Their footsteps and voices echoed throughout.

She turned to face him. But before she could speak, his hands were on her face, his mouth claiming hers like he hadn't kissed her in weeks. She gasped into it — surprised, overwhelmed — and his tongue swept into her mouth like it belonged there.

He kissed her like he meant to unmake her.

And she let him.

Her hands slid up his chest, fisting in the collar of his shirt. Her knees weakened. He caught her waist, pressed her against the wall. The hard line of his body pinned her in place.

When he broke the kiss, she was trembling.

"You kept your legs open for me," he said.

She nodded, panting. "Yes."

"That was brave."

"Was it?"

His mouth brushed her neck. "It was obedience. That's what I want."

Her knees buckled again. "Jake…"

He pulled back slightly, just enough to look in her eyes.

"You remember what I told you in the restaurant?"

Rainey swallowed. "Yes."

He nodded toward the center of the room — a soft leather couch, wide and deep.

"Go stand in front of it."

She moved. Barefoot now. Heart racing. Skin tingling with awareness.

She stood where he'd indicated, the city lights outside casting faint silver shapes on the walls.

He circled her once. Then stood in front of her.

"Take off your dress."

Her fingers moved instantly to the zipper at her side. But they fumbled.

Jake stepped closer. "No rush," he said. "Take your time. I'm not going anywhere…and neither are you."

That was the most dangerous thing he'd said all night. Because she wanted him to mean it.

The zipper came down. The dress slid off her shoulders, whispering to the floor.

She stood in nothing but the tiny lace panties she'd worn for him.

Jake took a step back.

His gaze moved down her body — slowly — like he was memorizing her piece by piece.

Not as a man who wanted to devour her. As a man who intended to own her.

"You have no idea what you do to me," he said.

She shifted, self-conscious.

His voice sharpened. "Don't hide from me now."

She stopped moving.

"I could worship you like this forever."

Then, softly: "Turn around."

She did.

He stepped behind her and traced a line down her spine with one finger. She shivered.

"Every inch of you," he said. "Is mine to learn."

She swallowed hard.

"Do you want me to learn you, Rainey?"

"Yes."

"Say it properly."

"Yes, Jake. I want you to learn me."

He pressed a kiss between her shoulder blades.

"Lie down."

She did.

The leather of the couch was cool beneath her skin. Jake knelt beside it.

She didn't open her legs. Not this time. He hadn't told her to.

Instead, she looked at him. Waiting.

He smiled, just faintly. "Already learning. I like that."

His hand slid to her thigh. He kissed her stomach again. Lower.

Then he hooked two fingers at the side of her panties and paused.

"Tell me you want me to take them off."

Rainey's breath caught.

"I want you to."

He raised an eyebrow.

She flushed.

"I want you to take them off, Jake."

He slipped them down — slow, deliberate, reverent. And dropped them to the floor.

She lay there — bare, open, shaking.

He didn't move between her legs.

He pressed one hand flat on her stomach and held her still.

"Tonight you're going to make a very big mess in my house," he whispered. "You're going to feel everything I give you. And you're going to ask before I take more."

Rainey's eyes filled with tears.

"Yes," she whispered.

"Yes what?"

"Yes, Jake."

He leaned in and whispered, "That's my girl."

And then, the world began to disappear.

Chapter Thirteen

THE TREMBLE

The first time Jake truly touched her — not just with his hands, but with full intent — she forgot how to breathe.

It wasn't just the brush of skin or the press of his body. It was the weight of his focus. The deliberate slowness. The devastating calm and the dominating confidence in the way he moved.

She lay stretched out on the couch, bare beneath the low light, her legs parted only slightly, heart pounding against the back of her ribs. The city lights poured in through the windows, silver and silent. But inside, everything buzzed — heat and tension and anticipation thick in the air.

Jake didn't rush. He never did. That was what undid her most.

He sat beside her — not over her, not looming — just there. Steady. Present. One hand pressed flat against her stomach, anchoring her. The other trailed down the inside of her thigh, slow as honey, teasing but never taunting.

"You're already shaking," he murmured.

She nodded, her throat too tight to form words.

"Good," he said, voice like warm smoke. "That means you're still with me."

His fingers hovered just shy of the place she needed him most. She was slick, aching, open for him, but he didn't touch her there. Not yet.

"You're going to let me take my time," he continued. "No rushing. No hiding. You'll feel every second of what I give you."

Rainey's eyes fluttered closed.

"Look at me."

The command was soft — not barked, not harsh — but it pulled her back like a leash around her heart. She opened her eyes immediately, locking onto his.

"Keep your eyes on me."

She whimpered.

He leaned down and kissed her, mouth soft at first, then deeper, coaxing her lips open until his tongue slid against hers in slow, drugging strokes. Her fingers gripped the couch cushions. She moaned into his mouth, trying to lift her hips for more, but Jake pressed her down again with the hand still flat on her stomach.

"Not yet."

"Please…"

"Not yet, Rainey."

Her entire body was trembling, her skin alive and on fire. She didn't just want his touch — she craved his *permission*. That was the part she hadn't expected. The part that scared her.

And thrilled her.

Jake moved lower. He kissed the hollow of her throat. The swell of her breasts. He paused at each nipple, tracing lazy circles with his tongue before sucking her into his mouth, one side at a time, making her cry out softly, over and over.

She was unraveling.

He moved lower.
Down her belly.
Across her hips.

Then he paused again. Looked up at her — steady, quiet, consuming.

"Open your legs for me."

She obeyed. No hesitation.

He slid his hands beneath her thighs and spread her open, deliberate and slow, holding her in place like she was made of something rare.

And then his mouth was on her.

Rainey arched off the couch with a strangled sound. His tongue moved over her, around her, *inside* her — licking, sucking, devouring — each movement expertly restrained, as though he wanted to worship, not finish.

She moaned, high and breathless, fingers digging into the cushions as he held her down with both hands.

Jake didn't speak. He didn't need to. His mouth said everything — his tongue coaxing her open, his lips vibrating with low moans against her most sensitive places.

He worked her like a song he already knew by heart.

Rainey bucked beneath him. Her breath faltered, fragile and trembling. She was close. So close. But still...

He pulled back slightly, lips slick and glistening.

"Ask me."

She blinked, dazed. "W-what?"

"Ask me to make you come."

Her face flushed. Her lips parted.

"Jake..."

"Say it."

A beat of silence. Then her voice — broken and breathless.

"Please... please make me come."

He smiled — dark and low.

"You belong to me."

Then he dove back in — harder, deeper, faster — and this time he slid one thick finger inside her as he sucked hard on her clit.

Rainey shattered.

She came with a sharp cry, her thighs clamping around his head, back arching so high it felt like flight. Her body pulsed, wave after wave, and Jake never stopped. He held her through it, licking and stroking her until she whimpered and twitched and begged for breath.

But he didn't stop there.

Every time she thought it was over, he began again — his mouth moving over her slick heat, his fingers curling inside her, his voice low in her ear:

"Again."
"Let go."
"That's it, baby. That's my girl."

She lost track of how many times she came.
Three?
Four?
More?

Her body writhed. Her moans became cries. Her cries became sobs. And still he didn't stop. Not until her voice broke and her thighs trembled and her chest heaved like she'd run for miles.

"Look at me," he said once, his voice sharp enough to cut through the haze. "You're not hiding from this."

She did.

Tears streaked down her temples, lips parted, whole body flushed and undone.

"You're going to come for me again," he whispered.

She whimpered, shaking her head.

"You can." His voice darkened. "And you *will*."

And she did.
She came so hard her cry became something primal — a sound she'd never made before, not even in the darkest hours of grief or love or pleasure. Her body seized, spasmed, opened.

And Jake held her through it all.

He slid back, breath heavy, eyes gleaming.

She was limp. Bare. Drenched in sweat and tears and the juices of her own pleasure.

Jake ran a slow palm down the center of her stomach, smearing the evidence of her release across her skin. Then up — over her ribs, her breasts, even her throat.

"Mine," he whispered.

Rainey could barely speak. She didn't need to. Her body was his answer.

He kissed her again, transferring the taste of her onto her lips. She melted beneath him, fingers weakly clutching his shoulders, thighs still trembling.

"Jake…" she gasped.

He pulled back just enough to look in her eyes.

"Say what you want."

"I want you to…" she swallowed hard. "I want you to fuck me. *Hard*. Please, Jake. I need it."

Something shifted behind his eyes.
Something animal.

He didn't speak.

He stood. Unbuckled his belt. Unzipped. Freed himself. And knelt between her thighs.

One brutal, perfect thrust.

She gasped — air knocked from her lungs.

Jake groaned — low and guttural. "Fuck, Rainey—"

She was so damn tight. So wet. So perfect.

He thrust again…more controlled, so he wouldn't explode.

But there was no way to stop the eruption her body had started.

That *grip*, the sound of her voice, the way she trembled beneath him — it all crashed into him like a tidal wave.

His hips locked. His breath caught.

He came with a force that stole his balance, his control, everything.

"Jesus—" he groaned into her shoulder as he buried himself deep, pulse after pulse rocking through him, her name falling from his lips like prayer.

When he finally collapsed over her, sweat-slick and shaking, she held him — hands cradling his back, fingers in his hair.

They stayed like that.
Breathless.
Silent.
Together.

Not because they had to.
But because they *couldn't* let go.

And that — that was the most terrifying part of all.

Chapter Fourteen

THE GAP

Rainey

The morning smelled like coffee and the quiet hum of something safe.

She stood wrapped in Jake's arms, her cheek pressed to his bare chest, listening to his heartbeat — slow and steady, like everything in him was built to calm storms.

He didn't rush her.
He didn't pull away.
He just held her like they'd done this a hundred times. Like this wasn't new. Like it wasn't terrifying to both of them.
But it was.

Rainey wasn't used to feeling tethered to anything but grief. Her days had been measured in numbness and survival. But now…
Now she stood in a stranger's kitchen wearing nothing but his warmth and the memory of what they'd shared the night before. And somehow, it felt more like home than anything she'd known in two years.

Jake's hands slid down her back, steady and slow.
"How are you feeling?" he asked against her hair.
She exhaled. "Incredible. Exhausted. Confused."
He smiled into her shoulder. "Sounds about right."

They stood like that for a few more minutes before Jake pulled back slightly, just enough to look into her eyes.

"You hungry?"
She nodded. "Starving."
"Let me feed you, then."

He made her eggs.
Scrambled, fluffy, cooked in butter. Toast, slightly burned. Coffee refilled without asking. He moved through the kitchen like a man who didn't need permission — not in arrogance, but in confidence.

Rainey sat at the counter in one of his flannel shirts, legs curled under her, watching him. She felt the hum of her body still responding to him, not from lust alone — though that was there too — but from something deeper. Reverent, almost.

She realized then how much she'd missed this kind of intimacy — the ordinary kind. Not the touches or the moans, but the moments in between. The quiet that didn't need to be filled.

Jake plated the food and set it down in front of her, then poured himself more coffee. He leaned on the counter beside her, his forearm brushing hers.

They ate in silence for a few minutes, and it wasn't awkward. It was comfortable — like the space between them had already been lived in.

Then he asked it.
"You have a son, right?"

She paused, fork halfway to her mouth.
"Yes. Dillon. He's fourteen."

Jake nodded, like the name settled something in him.
"You talk about him like someone who matters."

Rainey's throat tightened.
"He's extraordinary. He's everything."

Jake didn't respond right away. He took a sip of his coffee. Then: "He's your number one priority?"

She looked up, caught off guard by the gentleness in his tone.
"Yes," she said. "But more than that. He's everything. I love him more than life." Her voice cracked. "He's... different, strong.

Smarter than me – in a lot of ways. Quiet, but he notices *everything.*"

She put her cup down and looked directly at Jake.

"He watched his dad die right in front of him and still got up the next morning and hugged me like I was the one who needed saving."

Jake's jaw flexed.

Rainey looked down at her plate, her appetite dimming.
"I gave Shane CPR for eighteen minutes," she said softly. "Dillon was right there. I'm not sure how long or how much he witnessed, but I know the anguish and the shock."

Jake didn't move.

She swallowed hard. "There's something about knowing your child experienced that kind of trauma…" She again stared straight at him, "It changes who you are."

Jake put his hands across hers. "I believe that."

Rainey looked at him. "And you mentioned you have kids?"

He nodded once. "Six."

She almost spit out her coffee. Her eyes widened. "Six?"

"Scattered," he added. "Most are grown. Different moms. Most of them lived with me, but they've kinda moved on now. All but my youngest." He grinned, "Standard visitation. "

She didn't press. Didn't judge.
Instead, she said, "Oh…well, I love kids."

Jake gave a big smile. "Me too."

Another silence.
Then he said, "But I see that bond you have with your son. And if I ever got close to something like that again… I think I'd protect it with everything I had."

Her chest tightened.
He wasn't talking about fatherhood.

He was talking about them.
About her. About Dillon. About wanting to be part of that world.

Rainey blinked hard, the emotion rising too fast, too thick.
Jake reached across the counter and took her hand.

"Don't run from this," he said gently.

"I'm scared."

"So am I."
She looked up.

"But I'd rather be scared with you," he said, "than numb without you."

Later that morning, they moved to the couch — not to touch, not to seduce, but to rest. She lay curled against him, her head on his chest, his arm around her shoulders.

The city buzzed beyond the windows, but inside, everything felt still.

She closed her eyes.

"Jake?"

"Mm?"

"You're not just safe. You make me feel... wanted. Like I'm not something broken that needs fixing."

He kissed the top of her head.

"You're not broken," he said.

"Not even a little?"

"No," he whispered. "You walked through Hell, Rainey. You, Shane, Dillon. None of you asked for what happened to your family. But look at you. You're still here. You're rare. And I'm not letting you go."

She felt the words sink into her skin like warmth, like truth.

"I haven't let anyone in since him," she said after a long silence. "Not fully. Not this."

"I haven't either," Jake admitted. "Not like this."

He let his fingers trace light circles on her arm.
"I mean...yeah, I've had women in my life. Some for too long," He laughed. "But this... this already feels like more than anything I've known...it's all a bit surreal."

She tilted her head to look at him.
"Why me?"

He didn't hesitate.
"Because you're real. You didn't try to impress me. Because your grief didn't scare me. Because when I looked at you, I didn't see someone fragile. I saw someone fighting to live."

She blinked back sudden tears.

"And maybe because," he added, "you remind me of what it means to want something good. To believe that still exists."

They stayed like that for what felt like hours. Talking in quiet tones. Trading pieces of themselves — the ones they usually kept guarded.

Jake told her about his years in the Air Force, the faces he still saw in his sleep, the weight of decisions made in silence. He didn't talk about it to gain pity — just truth. Rainey listened without judgment. She took it in like someone who'd earned the right to hold his pain.

In return, she told him about the hospital. About the priest. And the autopsy. About the way Dillon hadn't cried for months — how he just stared out at the ambulance in disbelief, watching, his body huddled in total silence.

Jake didn't interrupt.

At one point, she said, "Sometimes I wonder if I'm healing, or just getting better at pretending."

He looked her straight in the eyes.
"You're healing."

And for once, she believed it.

When the sunlight stretched across the living room floor, Rainey sat up and pulled her knees to her chest. "I have to go soon," she said quietly.

Jake nodded. "I know."
He reached for her hand, held it in his lap. "But I don't want this to be a one-night memory."

"It's not," she said. "I couldn't forget this if I tried."

He hesitated. "Will I see you again?"

She gave him a small, tired smile. "You're going to see all of me, Jake. Eventually. Even the mess. Even the parts I hide."

"I want all of it," he said. "Even the mess. Just…don't change your mind — don't regret any of this tomorrow or after that — let's give this a chance."

She turned to him, took his face in her hands, and kissed him softly. "I'm not changing my mind. I just need to go slow."

Jake rested his forehead against hers.
"Then slow is what we'll do. But I'm not going anywhere."

And somehow, she knew he meant it.
Not possessively.
Not out of fear.
But a man who'd finally found something he wasn't willing to lose.

Chapter Fifteen

THE SWELL

Rainey

She was supposed to have left already, but she hadn't.
Neither of them left the house that day.
The outside world felt irrelevant. Too loud. Too fast.
There was no place safer than this — in the quiet between them, in the rhythm of Jake's breath and the weight of his presence.

After breakfast, they moved slowly, like the world had shifted and they hadn't quite adjusted to gravity. Jake pulled a thick throw blanket over the couch and turned on an 80's soft rock playlist that filled the space like velvet.
No TV. No distractions. Just soft music, warm light, and each other.

He didn't push for anything. He didn't expect it.
And that's what made Rainey ache for him more.

He kissed her shoulders when she passed him. Brushed his palm over her back when she reached for coffee. Touched her like a man who wasn't just hungry — but grateful.

She had never been touched like that.

It made her feel raw. Alive. Wanted.
Not for what she gave — but for who she was, simply breathing in his presence.

The hours drifted in quiet domestic rhythm, the inevitable separation left unspoken.

Jake didn't hover, but his presence lingered—in the room, in her chest, in the spaces between. And when he finally sat beside her on the couch again, stretching his arm behind her shoulders, she leaned into him like it was the most natural thing in the world.

His fingers brushed the side of her neck. Not possessive — but grounding.
And somehow, that touch said more than words ever could.

That night, as the sun slipped behind the buildings and the city fell into quiet darkness, Rainey found herself standing by the window, arms crossed, still wrapped in one of Jake's shirts.

The fabric was soft against her skin, but it was the scent that stirred her — the subtle blend of him: coffee, cedar, something masculine and clean. And as the flickering lights danced across the tops of distant buildings, a memory rose — uninvited but vivid — pulling her back to another skyline, another night, when love felt young and time felt infinite.

Atlanta. June. Neil Diamond at the Philips Arena...

They'd escaped their island home, dropped Dillon at her mother's with a weekend bag and a two-page long list of emergency numbers Rainey updated twice. Shane teased when he saw she'd circled the pediatrician's name, but then he checked and crosschecked the list – Three times.

God, he loved that boy.

By the time they reached Atlanta, the sky was ink-dark, and the neon signs from the hotels, bars and restaurants lit the inside of their SUV with pops of illuminating colors. She remembered the exact feel of her hand in his — the way he held it like he never got tired of touching her. They checked into a chic Airbnb penthouse – downtown, with a view that overlooked the glowing hum of the city.

She'd stood at the window then too, just like now — arms crossed, heart full. Only back then, there had been no grief threading itself through the stillness. No guilt drowning them in the sea of emotions between them. Just the sound of Shane humming behind her as he unpacked.

Always organized. Always precise.

"Two nights," he said, wrapping his arms around her waist. "Just us."

It was the first and last time they'd ever left town without Dillon.

That night, they walked to a charming little bistro tucked between a bookstore and a tattoo shop. She wore a black wrap dress and strappy heels. They ordered a bottle of wine and something with truffle oil.

She remembered him brushing a bit of pastry off the corner of her lip and the way his blue eyes twinkled every time he smiled.

She pressed her palm to the window, eyes tracing all of the hues of blue in the skyline beyond. She didn't hear him approach. She just felt him.

His chest pressed to her back. His hands slid around her waist. His chin rested on her shoulder.

"What are you thinking?" he murmured.

"That I don't know how to go back after this."

"I hope you don't," he said.

He kissed her neck — slow and deliberate.

"You gave yourself to me, Rainey. That doesn't just go away."

She felt her breath catch. Her thighs clenched. Her heart… opened.

"And I'm going to take care of you now," he added. "Whether you know how to need that or not."

She turned to face him, her voice almost too quiet. "I want that."

Jake studied her for a long moment, then stepped back and reached for her hand.

"Then come here."

He led her to the center of the room.
No couch. No bed.
Just open space.

Rainey stood there, trembling — not from fear, but anticipation.

Jake didn't speak right away.
He circled her slowly, eyes roaming her body with intention.

Then: "Take off the shirt."

She obeyed, sliding it off her shoulders until it fell to the floor.

He moved behind her again. She felt the warmth of his breath against her spine.

"Do you know what I see when I look at you?"

She shook her head.

"A woman who has lived through hell and still carries herself like something sacred."
His hand slid down the curve of her hip.
"A woman who wants to surrender, but doesn't quite believe she deserves the freedom that comes with it."

She swallowed, hard.

"But I'm going to teach you," he said softly. "I'm going to show you what it means to be kept."

Her knees nearly buckled.

He stepped in front of her.
"Tilt your chin up."

She obeyed.

"Open your mouth."

She did.

He leaned in — not to kiss, but to simply hover there, eyes locked on hers.

"You don't need to speak right now," he said. "Just feel."

Then he kissed her.
Not hungrily.
Not even tenderly.

Deliberately.

He kissed her like every second mattered. Like he was mapping her mouth. Like he was teaching her a language with his tongue and letting her forget every word she knew except him.

Rainey's body swayed toward his.
Jake caught her waist with one hand, his other moving slowly up the inside of her thigh.

"Do you know what I love most about you?" he murmured.

Her voice was breathless. "What?"

"You pay attention. You encapsulate everything."

He slid his fingers between her legs, found her already warm and waiting.
"You give me what I ask for."

His fingers stroked her once, then pulled back.
"But not until I say."

She whimpered, thighs clenching.
Jake smiled — not cruelly, but knowingly.

"You're going to stand here for me," he said. "Hands at your sides. Eyes on mine."

She nodded.

"You enjoy pleasing me. Letting me own every inch of you."

The words made her knees shake.

Jake dropped to his knees in front of her.

He kissed her belly. Her hips. The inside of her thigh.

But he didn't touch her center. Not yet.
He let her feel the absence.
Let her want.

Her breath turned ragged.

"I can't—"

"You can," he said, lips brushing her skin. "And you will."

She looked down at him — this strong, silent man kneeling at her feet, worshipping her with patience and possession.

And she realized she would give him anything.
Everything.

"Tell me you're mine," he whispered.

"I'm yours."

He kissed her once — soft and low — and then took her with his mouth like she was the only thing that had ever mattered.

She cried out.
Not from shock.
From relief.

He brought her to the edge again, slowly, methodically, praising her every time she whimpered.

"Just like that."
"Let go for me."
"There's my girl."

When she shattered, her whole body shaking, Jake stood and caught her.
Held her upright. Pressed her to his chest.

"You did perfect," he whispered into her hair.

"You... you didn't..."

"I didn't need to," he said.

She looked up at him, eyes wide.

"I needed *this*."

He held her face in both hands. "You don't understand, do you?"

"Understand what?"

"This isn't about me," he said. "I'm trying to keep you." He leaned close against her ear and whispered, "Forever."

The room was quiet. She lay curled in his arms again, her head resting over his heart. The playlist still echoed the rhythm of a beating heart in the background, a symphony of nostalgia and heartbreaking ballads wrapped around them like smoke.

Rainey whispered, "I'm afraid of what this means."

Jake didn't flinch. "So am I."

"But it's too late, isn't it?"

He nodded. "Way too late."

She laughed softly, and it sounded like surrender.

"Do you still want slow?" he asked, his fingers brushing her jaw.

She paused. "I want slow... but I want *you* more."

Jake kissed her again, slow and sure.

"You've got me," he said. "And the only place I want to be is wherever you are."

Chapter Sixteen
THE DRIFT

Rainey

She didn't cry when she left.

But something inside her tightened with every mile that pulled her farther from Jake.

Not panic. Not regret. Just this ache — deep and spreading — like the hollow between two ribs you never notice until something presses on it.

He'd walked her to the car just after noon. There was no grand goodbye, no desperate kiss. Just his arms around her, his hand cradling the back of her neck, and a promise whispered into her skin.

"I'll see you soon."

Rainey nodded, pressed her lips to his throat — that warm patch just beneath his jaw — and climbed into the driver's seat of her rental car.

He watched her as she backed out, and still, as she turned the corner. She knew because she kept checking the mirror — and he was there. Still standing in the street. Still wearing that quiet look in his eyes like she'd taken something from him without meaning to.

And maybe she had.

Because when she pulled into her driveway all those hours later, the world felt dimmer.

She killed the engine, sat in silence, and stared at the house — her house — like it belonged to someone else.

The porch swing Shane had installed. The raised flower beds she'd once cared for with pride. The wind chimes that hadn't been replaced since the last storm. It was all still here. Familiar.
And yet...

She wasn't.
Not the version of herself that used to call this place home.
Not the woman who measured life in dinner plans, laundry loads, and bedtime kisses.
Not the hollow widow she'd become, either — the one who moved through grief like fog.

Who was she now?

She stepped out, grabbed her bag, and barely made it to the front steps before the door swung open.

"Mom!"

Dillon stood in the doorway — lanky, barefoot, the cuffs of his hoodie pushed halfway up his forearms. His hair had grown too long again, that mop of sun-kissed brown curling at the edges, and Rainey felt her breath catch.

Because God, she'd **missed** him.

The truth hit her like a wave — she hadn't just missed him these past two days.
She'd been missing him for *years*.

While folding his laundry. While watching movies together. While tucking him in. Even while standing right in front of him and seeing that same, beautiful, hopeful smile.

They shared a house, shared meals, shared long stretches of quiet — but somewhere along the way, she shut down.

Grief had built walls where comfort used to live.
And now, standing in front of him, she felt the weight of everything they'd lost — not just Shane, but pieces of themselves. Pieces of each other. Pieces of their lives – past, present and future.

And she wanted them back.
All of them.

"Hey, sweetheart," she whispered, voice thinner than she meant it to be.

Dillon stepped aside, and Rainey dropped her bag and wrapped her arms around his shoulders. She didn't squeeze too tight. This wasn't her little boy anymore. But still — she needed this. Needed to feel him there. Needed *him* to feel *her*. Solid. Real.

And she just *held* him.

Dillon hugged her back without hesitation. He didn't shift or squirm. They both just held on.

When she pulled back, his face was unreadable. "Did you eat?" she asked.

"Pizza. And cereal."

She made a face. "Breakfast of champions."

He grinned. "It worked." Then, more softly, "Did you cry?"

Her smile faltered. "What?"

"While you were gone. Did you cry?"

She blinked. "Why would you ask that?"

Dillon looked away, kicking lightly at the corner of the doormat. "I know you, Mom." He hesitated. "I just hoped something good would happen – Like a real vacation. Away from feeling sad."

Rainey's chest cracked open.

She stepped forward again and cupped his cheek.
"It was... something I didn't know I still needed."

Dillon nodded, slow and serious, like he understood more than she said.
"You look different," he murmured.

"Different how?"

He studied her for a moment.
"I don't know. Just different."
Then, a small grin. "In a good way.

That night, after a quiet dinner and a few rounds of folding laundry together, Rainey stood in the shower and let the water dance over her shoulders.

She tilted her head back and closed her eyes, trying to let the warmth sink deeper than skin. But her body remembered Jake too vividly to rest.

Every mark he left still lingered — a bruise on her hip, a soreness between her thighs, a faint scrape on her rib from where his stubble rubbed against her too long.

But more than that, her body remembered the way he held her after. The weight of his arms. The warmth of his mouth. The steady rhythm of his breath when she curled into him, half-asleep, half-undone.

She had missed what it meant to be touched like that.

Jake hadn't taken from her.
He hadn't rushed.
He hadn't even expected.

He had *received* her.

And now, standing in the steam of her own bathroom, she felt more naked than when she'd taken off her clothes.

She missed him.

Not just the sensuality.
Not even just the touch.
She missed the way he watched her — like she wasn't broken at all.

She stepped out of the shower, toweled off in silence, and slipped into the soft gray shirt she'd "accidentally" packed. His shirt. The one that smelled like cedar and laundry soap and the base of his throat.

She crawled into bed, pulling the blankets to her chin, phone untouched beside her.
She didn't text him.

She didn't need to.

Because two minutes later, her phone buzzed.

Jake:
Did you make it?

Rainey:
Home. Showered. Missing you terribly.

Jake:
You're not sleeping alone in that bed. Not really.

Rainey:
I know.

A pause. Then:

Jake:
Touch yourself if you need to. But not before you ask me.

Her breath caught.

Heat curled low in her belly. Not just arousal — control. Ownership. Presence.

He was still with her.

Even from miles away, he held the reins.

And she had no intention of letting go.

Jake

He stared at the ceiling.
Motionless.

The house was too quiet.
The bed bitter without her.

He hadn't undressed. He hadn't moved. He lay on top of the covers like he was holding vigil.

Jeans still on. One arm behind his head. The other clutching the pillow she'd slept on.

She'd left that morning. Ten hours ago.

And yet… it felt like days.

Her scent was still on his skin. Vanilla. Sweat. A whisper of lavender.
But the sheets were empty, and the space beside him was silent.

His body ached — not from exertion, but from absence.

He let his eyes fall shut, but his mind kept playing her like a reel:

The way she trembled when he whispered, *good girl.*
The way she shattered in his arms, moaning his name.
The weight of her head on his chest, her breath fanning across his sternum.

But it wasn't the sex that haunted him.

It was her silence.

The kind of silence that meant trust. That meant safety.

She hadn't just given him her body.
She gave him her stillness.

And now he couldn't stop hearing it — the way she moved through the room, the way she hummed in the shower, the soft laugh when he burned the toast that morning.

It was burned on purpose, kind of.
He just wanted to make her smile.

He looked at his phone again.

Read her texts for the sixth time.

Home. Showered. Missing you terribly.

He should've called. Should've told her everything he was feeling.

But he didn't.
Because this wasn't about chasing.
Not anymore.

This was different.

For once, he wasn't fighting to earn something.
He was being *invited*.

And Jesus, he didn't know how long it would last, but he knew this:

If she called him right now and told him to come, he'd grab his keys and not even stop to put on socks.

He'd drive like the road belonged to him.
Because there was no question: Rainey was more than a beautiful distraction.
She was *the answer.*

To **everything** he thought was gone inside of him – the part that still believed in building something worth protecting.

He exhaled sharply, jaw tight, chest tighter.

He wasn't going to beg.
Wasn't going to push.

But soon...
Very soon...

He was going to need to see her again.

Because without her?

He didn't recognize himself anymore.

And he wasn't sure he could — or wanted to — find his way back to where he'd been for so long.

Chapter Seventeen

THE LIGHTHOUSE

Rainey

The house was quiet.

Not the silence of loneliness. Not the kind that clawed at her after Shane died, when even the creak of the floorboards felt like an echo of what used to be.

This was different.

Dillon was asleep. She could hear his soft breathing from down the hall — even, steady, the way only children and the truly unburdened could breathe.

She sat on the couch in the dark, wrapped in Jake's shirt like it was armor and memory all at once. It swallowed her — the sleeves draping past her hands, the hem skimming her bare thighs — and yet somehow, it fit her in all the ways that mattered.

It still smelled like him — soap, cedar, something warm and masculine that made her throat tighten every time she inhaled.

She hadn't turned on the lamp. The room was lit only by the dim halo of a streetlight pouring in through the window, casting long and welcomed shadows on the wall.

She didn't hear herself crying until she felt the damp warmth slide down her cheek.
There was no sob, no noise. Just the quiet ache that had lived inside her for nearly two years.

Only now, it had shifted.

The infinity of grief hadn't left her — but something else had risen alongside it.
Hope.

And hope, she realized, was more terrifying than grief.
Because it asked something of her.
It demanded faith.

Jake's last text still sat open on her screen:
Touch yourself if you need to. But not before you ask me.

It made her pulse race.
Made her thighs press together.
Made something stir low in her belly that she hadn't let herself feel in a long time.

But she didn't reply.
Not because she didn't want to.

Because she didn't know if she *should*.

Her world had changed over the weekend.
Not in one dramatic, cinematic sweep — but in a series of quiet moments: a look, a kiss, the weight of his hand at the back of her neck when he whispered, *I'm not going anywhere.*

Now she was back in the house she'd built with Shane. Back in the routines she'd duct-taped together with love and guilt for nearly two years.

And somehow, it all felt too small for the thing growing inside of her.

Jake doesn't fit in this world, she thought.
But he's the only thing that makes it feel alive again.

She walked quietly to Dillon's door and peeked in.

He lay curled on his side, the blankets kicked off, one arm bent under the pillow, mouth slightly open. The moonlight from his window cut a soft angle across his face, illuminating the baby cheeks that still clung to his jaw when he slept.

She stood there for a long time.
Watching.
Remembering.

This bed. This room. This boy she'd run back to a million times after Shane collapsed on the hotel floor. She watched.

They returned home, her knees still raw from the Berber carpet, her arms still trembling from compressions and hands desperately clasped in frantic prayer. In the darkness, she developed the quiet obsession of checking to make sure Dillon was still breathing. Night after night, she crept into his room, lay beside him, placing her hand gently on his chest, carefully nestling her cheek close enough to feel his breath.

She never told anyone.
Not even Dillon.

For six months, she'd slept next to that boy — sometimes in the bed, sometimes on the floor.
She'd told herself it was for him.
But it wasn't.
It was for her.

Because if he stopped breathing too, she needed to be the one who knew.
She needed to try.

Now, standing in that same doorway, Rainey felt the weight of what she was about to do.
Invite someone into this sacred space.
Not just her home.
But her son's life.

And it terrified her.

She made a cup of chamomile tea she didn't drink.
Sat barefoot on the back steps, letting the cool night air sting her skin.
Her legs were bare. Jake's shirt still clung to her body, the hem heavy from humidity.

She stared at the shadows stretching across the yard — the wind brushing softly through the crepe myrtles Shane planted, the fence creaking slightly — and let her thoughts drift back to him.

His hands.
His voice.
The way he'd looked at her when she came undone in his arms.

But more than that — she remembered his stillness.
How he'd let her fall apart and didn't flinch.
How he held space for her grief without trying to fix it.

He didn't want to rescue her.
He wanted to *see* her. He wanted to *share* in their grief.

And somehow, that was more dangerous than anything else.

She thought about the way he'd talked about Dillon — not with forced kindness, not with obligation.
But with reverence.

If I ever got close to something like that again… I think I'd protect it with everything I had.

That line haunted her.
Because she *believed* him.

But believing him didn't erase the risk.

What if it scared Dillon?
What if Jake got too close, too fast?
What if he fell in love with this quiet, broken family and then —

And then what?

Didn't wake up?

Just like Shane.

And she had to bury someone all over again.
Had to watch her son lose *again*.

And herself – she'd have to die all over again.

She pressed her palms to her face, heart pounding.

This wasn't just about caution.
This was about fear.

Because falling in love with Jake didn't feel like climbing.
It felt like *leaping*.

And she didn't know if she could survive another fall.

The next morning, Dillon noticed.

Of course he did.
He always did.

She was at the stove, making eggs that no one asked for, humming without realizing it.

He looked at her over his cereal bowl, spoon halfway to his mouth. "You're different again," he said.

She turned. "Oh?"

"You look like you're trying not to smile."

Rainey tilted her head. "That obvious?"

He shrugged. "Do I need to know something?"

She paused. Then sat at the table across from him. She took both of his hands in hers, "I met someone, honey."

Dillon didn't react. He just listened and stared into his cereal. "He's really interesting," she added. "It's... intense."

He looked up.
"Do I know him?"

"No."

"Are you going to introduce me?"

She smiled faintly. "Eventually. But only when you're ready."

Dillon reversed his hands to take hers.
"Mom?"

"Yes?"

"I hate seeing you alone. I want you to have a life and be happy."

Her breath caught. "I know."

"But I also don't want just anyone…like – don't be with anyone who doesn't appreciate you or really make you happy. Someone who doesn't treat you like…you deserve."

She blinked. "What makes you think I'd ever choose someone like that?"

He looked at her with eyes that were all Shane — clear, steady, serious beyond his years.
"Because you've been through so much. I just worry you might not always see clearly."

She reached across the table and took his hand.

"This one… he makes me feel seen. Valuable. Stronger. Not smaller."

Dillon was quiet for a long moment.
Then he nodded.
"Good," he said simply. "So what are we waiting for? When do I get to meet him?"

Just like that.

And something broke open inside her.

Not in a painful way. But in the way a door opens when you didn't realize you'd locked it from the inside.

Because this boy — her son — had always been her quietest strength.
He never rushed her grief. Never made her feel like she had to hide it.
He never asked her to move on.

But he'd *wanted* her to.
For a long time now.

He had lived through the same storm, watched the same darkness take hold of the woman who once lit up every room — and he was ready to see her shine again.

And maybe, finally… she was too.

That night, Rainey stood in front of the bathroom mirror, wrapped in a towel, phone in her hand.

Jake hadn't messaged her since the night before.

He was giving her space.
Respecting the quiet.

But the quiet didn't feel peaceful anymore.
It felt *chaotic.*

Because she didn't want distance.
She wanted his hands. His voice in the hallway. His laugh in the kitchen. His boots beside the front door.

She didn't want a man who lived in another state and came and went with the seasons.
She wanted permanence.
Not in theory.
In proximity.

She opened her phone and stared at their thread.

Then, slowly, she typed:

Rainey:
I want to see you.

The dots appeared immediately.

Jake:
When?

She hesitated. Then:

Rainey:
Soon. But don't get a hotel.

Jake:
What do you want?

Her heart pounded.

She typed slowly, deliberately:

Rainey:
I want you to come home to me.

The typing bubble reappeared almost instantly.

Jake:
Tell me when.

She stared at the screen.

Then typed:
Not yet. But soon.

His reply came in less than a second:

Jake:
I approve this.

She smiled.

Then cried.

Not because she was scared.
Not because she regretted it.

But because, somehow, that simple phrase — *I approve this* — was the exact permission she didn't know she'd needed.

It wasn't a demand.
It wasn't a plea.

It was trust.
And the beginning of *everything*.

Chapter Eighteen

THE LOOMING

Rainey

It began with the sheets.

She hadn't expected it to matter. But as she stood in the doorway of her bedroom, sunlight soft on the wood floors, the bed seemed... different.

Too made. Too untouched.

Too much like a shrine.

It had been hers and Shane's. For almost two decades.

The headboard was still the same — smooth dark oak with a scratch near the top where Dillon had crashed a toy Thomas the Train into it when he was three.

Nothing had been replaced after Shane died. It all remained unchanged: the mattress, the pillows, the lamp he always turned off last, the drawer where his reading glasses still lived, untouched.

Even the photo of the three of them at the beach — Dillon still in diapers, her hair sunlit and tangled, Shane proudly beaming with Dillon in one arm and the other around her waist.

They had looked so young.

Beautiful. Naïve.

Innocent in the way only people are when they believe they have time.

She crossed the room slowly and sat on the edge of the bed.
It didn't creak.
That felt wrong too.

Everything was too still. Too silent.
Like it was waiting for her to make a choice.

Jake's words echoed in her mind:
Tell me when.

She wanted him here.
Not just in her bed.
In her *life*.

But this room… this house… it still bore the weight of a love she had buried, not willingly.

And the thought of laying with another man in this bed — of replacing one kind of warmth with another — felt like tearing open a seam that had never fully healed.

She spent the morning cleaning.

Not because the house was dirty.
Because she needed to move.

She washed the bedding.
Vacuumed the hall.
Sorted the junk drawer she hadn't opened in two years.
Wiped down doorknobs and baseboards.
Reorganized Dillon's closet.

She needed to be doing something — anything — that kept her hands busy while her heart battled her head.

But by noon, the house smelled like lemon and soap, and she was left with herself.

She stood in the bedroom again, holding a clean stack of sheets.
She stared at the bare mattress for a long time.

Then, carefully, she opened the bottom drawer of Shane's nightstand.

His favorite T-shirt.
A book he never finished.

A leather watch he'd meant to repair.
And a sealed envelope labeled in his handwriting: *Rainey, just in case.*

She didn't open it.
Not yet.

She lifted the shirt to her face and inhaled.
There was nothing left of his scent.

She folded it slowly and placed it back inside, then closed the drawer and stood.

Her voice came quiet.

"I'll always love you."

She wasn't sure who made the sound — Shane, herself, or the memory that filled this room like dust.

"But I need to live now."

Her hands trembled as she pulled the fresh sheets over the bed. Not to erase him.

To include him — in the version of her that survived.

Later that evening, Dillon came home from a friend's house.

Rainey was in the kitchen when he walked in, kiss her on the cheek and pulled out his AirPods.

"Smells clean," he said.

She glanced up. "That's either a compliment or an insult."

"It's both!"

He smiled, pulled a soda from the fridge and leaned against the counter, watching her.

"You okay, Mom?"

Rainey dried her hands on a towel and turned to face him.

"I'm thinking about inviting him over."

Dillon didn't flinch. "The guy?"

She nodded, "Jake."

"Is he your boyfriend now?"

The question caught her off guard.

"I don't know what we are."

"Do you love him?"

Her mouth opened. Then closed. Then opened again. "Yes."

Dillon looked down, chewing his bottom lip.

"Are you okay with that?" she asked.

He was quiet for a while.

Rainey stepped forward and cupped his face.

"I will love your father every minute of every day for the rest of my life. NOTHING will change that."

He nodded. "Mom, I already know that," he said. "I'm okay. I'm just…. happy."

She blinked. "Happy?"

"You deserve it more than anyone I know," he said. "Just… don't push him away. You gotta go for it."

After he went to bed, Rainey sat in the living room with a cup of tea, staring out at the darkness.

The lights were off.
The house was still.
And whispering through the silence, Dillon's words surged through her like a sudden storm.

This kid loved her.
He wanted her to leap – not tiptoe.

She held her phone in her lap.
Her thumb hovered over the screen.
She knew what she needed to say.

She typed slowly:

Rainey:
I want you to come over.

She didn't send it right away.
Instead, she whispered to the night:

"I love you, Shane."

Then she pressed send.

Jake

He stared at her text for a long time.

I want you to come over.

It should have been simple.

But nothing about it felt small.
It felt final. Groundbreaking.

Like someone had handed him a key to a door he never thought
he'd be invited to knock on, let alone step through.

He hadn't moved for ten full minutes.

Still sitting on the edge of the bed.
Elbows on his knees.
Her message glowing on the phone in his palm.

His pulse thudded slow and heavy.
He read it again.
And again.

He wasn't used to being wanted like this — not in a way that felt
sacred.
Not in a way that came with a child in the next room and old
ghosts in the walls.

This wasn't sex.
This wasn't about claiming territory.

This was about being *trusted*.

And that wrecked him.

He moved like he was heading into a mission.

Shower. Shave. Clean clothes. Packed. Tactical calm.

But under it — under the discipline and habit — was something deeper.
Something raw.

He looked at his reflection and barely recognized it.

Not because he looked different.
But because for the first time in years, he wasn't gearing up to protect himself.
He was gearing up to *offer* himself.

And it scared the hell out of him.

He grabbed a shirt — plain black, clean lines — and stared at it before pulling it on.

He had no idea what to bring. Essentials. No overthinking.

He just got in his truck.

The drive was long. The sky dimmed into that indigo hour just before night.He leaned into the road, into the silence, remembering why and where he was going. But his chest stayed tight the entire time. He thought about her voice the night before.

About the ache in it. The courage it took to ask him into that space. Into her *life*.

And he thought about Dillon.

The boy he hadn't met yet, but already felt protective of.

Because he knew kids like that — kids who were quiet because the world had demanded too much of them too soon.

And he knew what it meant to want to protect someone like that... even if you weren't sure you deserved to.

Jake had seen his own children often.
Birthdays. Holidays. Summer stretches when schedules aligned.
Some had even lived with him for a while.

But it was always a battle.
Distance.
Bitterness.
Tension with their mothers — women who resented him for

working too much, for not loving *them* enough.
Women who weaponized his devotion.

He paid. He called. He showed up.

But still, he always felt like a man trying to hold water in cupped hands.
The love was there. But it slipped through.

And now?
He didn't know if he had anything left to give.

But Rainey made him want to try.

Because she didn't just *accept* him.
She *trusted* him. *She believed in him.*

She looked at him like he wasn't a mistake.
She let him lead.
Let him in.

And the thought of losing that — of screwing it up — made his hands sweat.

He pulled into her driveway just past dusk.
The porch light was on.

He sat there for a minute. Engine off. Fingers on the wheel.

Then he stepped out and walked to the door.

He didn't knock.

She opened it before he could.

She stood barefoot in the doorway, backlit by the soft light behind her, wearing jeans and a sweater that clung to her like second skin.

Her hair was down. A little tousled.

No makeup. No performance. Just Rainey.

And God, she was beautiful.

But more than that — she was *real.*
Completely, achingly real.
Standing in front of him like she hadn't just invited him into her

house…
But into her life.

"Hi," she said softly.

"Hi."

They just stood there for a beat.

Then she stepped forward, into his arms, and pressed her face to his chest.

And everything made sense again.

She let him in quietly.

The house smelled like coffee and lemon. Warm. Inviting.

There were photos on the wall — her, Dillon, Shane.

He paused at one:
A young Rainey laughing on a picnic blanket, her eyes wild with joy. Shane beside her, holding her hand.

Jake studied it.

"I left all the photos up," she said from behind him.

"You should," he said. "You don't have to explain that to me."

"I want to."

He turned.

"No, Rainey. You don't."

She stepped forward. "He's still… here. Not physically. But here."

Jake nodded. "And he should be. Don't let anyone change that."

"But you being here," she whispered, "doesn't take away from what he was."

He looked at her for a long moment.

"Doesn't take away from what I can be, either," he said. "I'll never be that guy."

Her eyes shimmered.

And just like that — something clicked.

He belonged here.
Not because he deserved it.
But because he was willing to *earn* it.

Chapter Nineteen
THE SHORE

Jake

He heard the footsteps before he saw him.
Not heavy. Not dragging.
Light, but purposeful — the kind that belonged to a kid who didn't stomp for attention or slink away to avoid it.

The kind that said:
I know you're here. And I'm coming anyway.

Jake stood in the living room, hands in his pockets, eyes tracing the photos on the wall as Rainey moved toward the hallway to meet her son.

"You sure you're ready for this?" she whispered.

Jake nodded once. "I've never been more sure of anything."

A moment later, Dillon stepped into view.

Fourteen, tall for his age, good-looking in a quiet way. Confident, but not loud.
Hair a little long.
Eyes sharp. Direct.
He wore an oversized T-shirt and gym shorts. Arms crossed, but not in defiance — just comfortably guarded.

Jake recognized the posture instantly.
He'd seen it before.
Worn it before.

It was the look he'd given his mother's new boyfriend at fourteen.
The one that said:
I'll let you stay. But I'll decide if you belong.

Dillon's gaze didn't waver. He walked forward, slow and deliberate, every inch of him tuned to observation.

Jake didn't smile too wide. Didn't reach out. Didn't talk too fast.

He just nodded, calm and measured.
"Hey, Dillon."

His voice was even — grounded, but gentle.

"Hello," the boy replied. "It's nice to meet you."

Jake hadn't offered a handshake.
But Dillon extended his anyway.

Polite. Assertive.
Not trying to impress — just meeting the moment like someone who understood what it meant to show up well.

Jake took it.
One firm shake. Then released.

They stood there for a beat — no awkwardness, no forced small talk.
Just the low hum of curiosity stretching between them.

Rainey stepped lightly into the space between them, her energy careful. Protective.

"I figured we'd eat out back. It's nice tonight."

Dillon smiled faintly and reached up to brush her shoulder.
"Sounds good, Mom."

Jake caught that moment.
That gentle, instinctive gesture.
Not performative.
But full of affection.

This wasn't a boy.

This was a young man.
One who loved his mother with his whole chest.
One who didn't waste words, but paid close attention.

And Jake understood that kind of love — because he felt it, too.

The patio was strung with café lights — warm and golden, swaying gently in the early evening breeze.

Rainey brought out plates of roasted chicken, herbed potatoes, and salad.
Dillon carried out the water pitcher, glasses, and silverware.

Jake waited.
He didn't rush to help or hover.

He waited until they were settled — letting the rhythm of their household shape his own entry into it.

Dillon sat across from him.
Shoulders relaxed. Eyes alert.

He didn't fidget.
Didn't retreat.
He just ate — quiet and steady. Watching.

Jake didn't take it personally.
He respected it.

This wasn't distrust.
It was diligence.

Halfway through the meal, Rainey excused herself to grab something from the kitchen.

The second she disappeared through the door, Dillon's fork paused.
His gaze lifted.

"So are you a cop?"

Jake met his eyes evenly. "Air Marshal."

"That's similar to a cop, right?"

Jake nodded. "Pretty much."

A pause. Dillon chewed. Swallowed.
Then:
"Have you ever shot anyone?"

Jake didn't blink.
"Yes."

Dillon's fork hovered in the air.
His eyes narrowed slightly.

"Did they die?"

Jake didn't look away.
"One did."

Silence.
It wasn't uncomfortable.
It was just… real.

Dillon sat back, set his fork down, and folded his arms across his chest.

"No hesitation in your response," he said. "Like someone who doesn't lie."

Jake shrugged. "Lying to a smart person is a waste of everyone's time."

Dillon tilted his head, a small smile twitching at the edge of his mouth.
"Is that how you see me?"

Jake sipped his water. "That's how you carry yourself."

Rainey returned a moment later, setting down a small bowl of dressing.

She looked between them.

Neither said a word.

But something had shifted.

After dinner, Dillon stood and began clearing plates.

Jake moved to help, but Rainey gently touched his wrist.

"Let him," she whispered. "He wants to."

So Jake sat back.

He watched the boy move — efficient, focused.
Stacking, rinsing, wiping down the counter like it was second nature.

Rainey sat beside him with a quiet sigh.

"You handled that well," she murmured.

Jake's eyes stayed on the kitchen.
"I didn't handle anything. I just let him meet me."

She turned toward him.

"You made it comfortable."

"I'll always make it comfortable where he's concerned."

She looked down, her lips pressed together.

Jake reached for her hand beneath the table.

She gripped his fingers.

"Thank you," she whispered.

"For what?"

"For caring about us. For caring about *him*."

Jake's voice was low, steady.
"He's not just your son, Rainey. He's part of you. I don't get to love you without loving him."

She blinked, overwhelmed by the weight of it.

And then Dillon's voice broke the quiet from the kitchen.

"You staying over?"

Rainey turned, startled.

Jake didn't hesitate.
"Only if it's okay with both of you."

A pause.

Then, from the sink — casual, but sincere:
"Yeah. I think you should."

Later, the house was dim and still.
Dillon was in his room.

Jake and Rainey curled together on the couch — her legs across his, her head tucked beneath his chin.

Neither of them spoke.
The silence was warm. Present.

Finally, she whispered, "You didn't try to win him."

Jake kissed the top of her head.
"I didn't come here to impress him."

She tilted her head up slightly.
"What did you come for?"

Jake looked down at her, his hand moving slowly along her back.

"To earn his trust."

She exhaled, her body softening against him.
"You're doing it."

He kissed her again.

"I'm going to do it every day."

Upstairs, Dillon lay awake.

He wasn't worried.
Not exactly.

But his mind was busy.

He'd seen the way Jake looked at his mom — not with pity, not with hunger, but with something protective.
Something grounded.

It wasn't just affection.
It was commitment.

And even though Dillon didn't know this man, not really, he knew the difference between someone *trying to be liked*...
And someone *trying to matter.*

He was still watching.
Still waiting.
Still measuring what this all meant.

But for the first time in a long time…

She wasn't sad and he wasn't so scared for her.

Chapter Twenty

THE QUELL

Rainey

She woke before anyone else.
The house was quiet — not hollow, but full.
Bathed in that bluish, silvery light that only comes just before sunrise, the kind that makes shadows softer and silence sweeter.

She sat at the edge of the bed, Jake's warmth still clinging to the sheets, the weight of his presence still pressed into the mattress beside her.

The scent of him lingered on her skin.
That clean, masculine blend of cedar and salt air and something darker — like coffee grounds and late nights.

It felt like a claim.
Not one taken.
One *offered*.

She pulled on a robe and crept barefoot into the kitchen, careful not to wake him or Dillon.

The air was cool. Clean.
Her body ached in the most comforting way — not from exhaustion, but from being *held*.
From being touched gently. From being wanted with intent.

She exhaled slowly.

It felt like magic.

Not fireworks. Not breathless urgency.
Just the slow, steady rhythm of something good.

She stood at the window and watched the sky shift in real time.
Watched the shadows pull back and the soft blue swell into streaks
of pale gold.

Two hummingbirds danced across the glass. Their wings a blur of
motion, their bodies still as breath.

She lifted her fingers as if to touch the pane — but stopped short.
She just smiled instead.

Last night had changed something.

Jake had met Dillon.

Not with performance.
Not with charm or forced connection.

Just steady honesty.
Just space.

He had treated her son like a person.
Not a child.
Not a complication.
Not a test.

And somehow, that had meant more to her than anything else he
could have done.

She put the kettle on the stove and stood in the stillness, her heart
calm in a way she didn't recognize — but welcomed.

This was the first time in a long time she wasn't bracing for
something to go wrong.
And that felt so right.

Jake appeared just as she poured the tea.

T-shirt. Sweats. Bare feet.
Hair slightly messy from sleep.

God, he was *all **man***. And so sexy.

But it wasn't just the body — though that alone was enough to make
the air tangle in her lungs.

It was the way he filled a room without trying.
The way his voice still rumbled low and rough from sleep.
The way the cotton of his shirt clung just slightly to the muscles beneath, and how even relaxed, his frame held a kind of quiet power — coiled, restrained, yet always ready to protect.

He moved with purpose, even when he wasn't moving for anything. And she felt it — in the way her thighs pressed instinctively together, in the flush that spread over her chest, in the way her breath came just a little quicker when he stepped closer.
This was the man who had touched her like she was sacred.
And made her come apart with a single word.

He didn't even notice the effect he had.
Didn't play it up. Didn't posture.
He was just himself. And that made it worse — and better.
Because her desire for him wasn't just about his body.
It was the ache that came from knowing that the same hands that cradled her face in silence had also held her down with reverent strength.
That the same mouth that whispered I love you had once demanded her surrender with a single command.

She watched him now — calm, sleepy, beautiful — and her body remembered everything.
Every kiss. Every growl against her ear. Every time he said her name like it was his.

He came closer, stepping behind her and wrapping his arms around her waist like he'd done it a thousand times.

"You're up early," he murmured into her neck.
"You look beautiful."

"I didn't want to miss this part."

"What part?"

"This. You. The morning. All of it."

He pressed a kiss to her temple.

"I could get used to this."

She smiled, eyes still on the window.
"You already are."

Dillon came down around eight.

He didn't say much at first — just a nod at Jake and a soft
"Morning" to his mom, followed by a kiss on her cheek.

He looked like a teenager again, not a soldier in a boy's body. Sleep
still clung to his face.

But when Jake offered him the plate of bacon before serving
himself, Rainey noticed the subtle shift.

A small thing.
But it mattered.

Respect, offered quietly.

They ate at the table.
Not rushed. Not awkward.

Just comfortably.

Dillon talked about a project he had for school — a historical
analysis paper. He wasn't animated, but he spoke with interest.

Jake listened.
Not distracted. Not half-engaged.
But fully present.

He asked a question.
Then another.

"Want help?" he said after a moment.

Dillon shrugged. "You into history?"

Jake smiled. "I've lived enough of it to be interested."

Dillon gave the ghost of a smile.
"I might have to take you up on it."

Rainey turned toward her coffee, blinking fast.
Because something opened in her chest so quietly, she almost didn't
notice.

Shane – a walking encyclopedia – full of interesting facts, figures, obscure timelines and random information — they came to him as naturally as breath.

Dillon came home with a school packet on World War II. The assignment seemed boring to him — dry textbook material. But Shane leaned forward at the kitchen table, eyes lit up like someone had handed him a mission. "Let me show you something," he'd said.

He opened his laptop, pulled up a colorized image of a young soldier kneeling beside a wounded friend on the beaches of Normandy. No blood. Just grit. Courage. History with a face.

The sound of Shane's voice echoed in her mind. The way he explained battles and borders. The cost of freedom. The quiet heroism of ordinary men. The way every name in a footnote had once been someone's son.

And now, in this moment — as Rainey stood near the counter, listening to Jake talk to Dillon about history with genuine interest, asking questions instead of giving lectures — she felt it.

A shift.

Not a replacement.

Not a replication.

But a continuation.

A new voice in the room.
A different kind of knowing.
A man who didn't carry encyclopedic facts — but carried weight.
Experience. Perspective.

The morning passed in soft waves.

Jake helped clean out and totally reorganize the garage — not because she asked, but because he saw her struggling with a broken bin and simply joined in.

She'd been meaning to do it for months, but couldn't find the energy.

They sorted holiday boxes.
Swept the corners.

He pulled down a dusty tote labeled *Spring decorations,* cracked the lid, and held up a faded wreath.

Rainey rolled her eyes. "Don't judge me."

"Too late," he said, grinning.

Dillon worked on his project at the kitchen table, earbuds in, but every so often, he'd glance toward the open garage door.

Just watching.
Measuring.

Jake didn't wave.
Didn't push.
He just kept working.

And Dillon just kept noticing.

At lunch, Jake offered to grill.

He stood on the back deck manning the gas grill like he was born to do it — relaxed, competent, calm.

Dillon hovered nearby, half-interested, half-playing it cool.

Rainey came out with plates and caught them mid-conversation.

"...Not a bad sear you've got there," Dillon said.

Jake raised an eyebrow.
"High praise?"

"Don't push it."

She didn't interrupt.

She just watched.

These two people — once strangers, once separate corners of her life — were slowly, wordlessly, making room for each other.

And she didn't even realize she was crying until she blinked and her vision blurred.

That afternoon, they went for a walk.

Just the three of them.

It was unseasonably cool for spring.
The air crisp, clouds stretched low across the sky like cotton pulled thin.

They walked the edge of the neighborhood park.

Dillon kicked at pinecones, a stick in his hand like some subconscious leftover from being younger.

Jake walked beside her, hand brushing hers occasionally — not gripping, not pulling, just a touch.

It wasn't loud.
It wasn't dramatic.

But it felt like *life*.

Something normal.
Something rare.

A group of older boys biked past, laughing too loud, shoving each other.

One shouted something crass — a joke, meaningless but sharp.

Jake didn't react right away.

But Rainey saw it — the way his jaw tightened.
The way his eyes flicked toward Dillon, then her.

And how he stepped slightly in front of them.
Not aggressively.
Not to make a scene.

Just instinctively.

Protectively.

Dillon noticed.

A few seconds later, when they were alone again, he asked, "You always do that?"

Jake looked over. "Do what?"

"Step in front."

Jake shrugged. "Only when something matters to me."

Dillon didn't respond.
But he didn't look away either.

He made mental notes.
Jake could tell.
And Jake didn't mind.

That evening, the house smelled like garlic and something warm.

Rainey made pasta, barefoot in the kitchen, music humming low in the background.

Jake watched her.

Dillon set the table without being asked.
Jake poured the drinks.

And it was just easy.

Not perfect.
Not polished.

But honest.
Kind.
Rooted.

They laughed at one point — over something dumb. A song lyric. A bad joke.

And Jake felt it in his chest.

That slow, steady unfolding of something permanent.

Later, after Dillon had showered and gone upstairs, Rainey and Jake sat curled on the couch, the room dim.

She was in his arms, her head on his chest.

His hands moved over her shoulders in slow, steady circles.

"Today felt so… good," she whispered.

"It felt *right*," he said.

She tilted her head back against him, eyes closed.
"He likes you."

Jake didn't smile.
He just nodded.

"I like him," he said.
"I'm here to give you both everything I've got."

Rainey turned, pulled him down beside her, and kissed him — not with urgency, but with that quiet devotion that only builds through presence.

"You already are," she whispered.

And for the first time in years...
She believed it.

Chapter Twenty-One

THE POSSESSION

Rainey

The house was still.

Not just quiet — but settled. Steeped in calm.

Dillon had spent the night with a friend from the neighborhood, one he'd met earlier that week. The air was warm, the dishes were done, and the rooms glowed with the soft hush of lamps dimmed low — like the day itself had been folded gently into the fabric of something new. Something sacred.

Rainey stood at the edge of the hallway, her fingers curled lightly around the doorframe. She could see Jake from where she was — stretched across the couch like he'd been born there, like his presence didn't disrupt the air but belonged to it.

He wasn't watching TV.
Wasn't on his phone.
Wasn't even looking her way.

He just waited. Still. Composed. Safe.

And that — more than anything — was what made her body ease.
He didn't pursue.
He invited.
And she answered.

"Come here," he said, his voice low, without turning around. Like he could feel her in the doorway. Like her soul had a sound he'd already memorized.

She smiled.

Then moved.

They didn't rush.

Not this time.
Not in this house.

There was no fevered push of clothing or reckless urgency. There was only closeness. Breath. Intention.

And the unspoken truth that this night — in her space, in her bed — would mean more than the others. This was her sanctuary. The house where she'd loved Shane, grieved him, raised her son, and spent so many nights frozen in sorrow.

Now, she was choosing to let someone else inside it.

Jake stood when she reached him. He took the cup from her hands — gentle, like it held more than tea — and set it aside. His fingers brushed hers, warm and steady, then traced the back of his knuckles along her cheek.

"You sure?" he asked.

She nodded. Her voice came softer than breath.

"Yes."

He held her gaze for another heartbeat — as if double-checking for hesitation, for fear — then threaded his fingers with hers and led her toward the bedroom.

Not with hunger.
With reverence.

Like even the walls needed time to adjust to his presence.

Inside, the room glowed faintly. The scent of lavender hung in the air, familiar and calming. Her robe was still on the hook. Her slippers still beside the nightstand.

It was all so ordinary.

And yet, nothing about this night felt ordinary.

Jake sat at the edge of her bed. His body relaxed, but his energy focused. He didn't undress. He didn't move fast. He just looked at her — really looked — like he was seeing not just her skin, but everything beneath it.

"You okay?" he asked.

Rainey stepped closer. She nodded.

"More than okay."

He reached for her hand and brought it to his mouth. Kissed her wrist. Then, without letting go, he kissed her forearm — a slow press of lips that sent a tremor through her knees.

"Are you comfortable with me in here?"

She leaned down until her breath brushed his lips.
"Very comfortable with you right here."

Jake smiled. That quiet, reverent smile. The one that made her forget everything before him.

"Then let's go slow."

He stood and stepped close, sliding his hands beneath the hem of her shirt. Not to undress her yet — not quite — but to feel her. His palms rested at her hips, warming the skin there. His thumbs traced soft circles as his mouth dipped toward her neck.

He kissed her jaw.
The corner of her mouth.
The slope where her collarbone met her shoulder.

Her chest rose suddenly, unsteady. Her eyes fluttered closed.

It wasn't just arousal.

It was awe.

Every kiss was permission.

Every touch asked a question and gave her the space to answer.

She reached for his shirt, lifting it slowly over his head. His chest rose as she peeled it away, revealing muscle shaped by years of use

— not sculpted for show, but earned. His body was firm, scarred, alive with story.

Her fingertips hovered at the lines on his shoulder. She touched them gently, reverently.

Jake didn't flinch.

He didn't explain them.

He just let her look.

Let her see him.

All of him.

"You're beautiful," she whispered.

He gave a quiet laugh — not dismissive, but disbelieving.

"That's your line."

"It's the truth."

He didn't answer. Just kissed her again — soft, open, unhurried — like he had all night and nothing else mattered.

And maybe he did.

Maybe they both did.

Because what came next wasn't sex.

It was something deeper.

It was a return.

A reclamation.

A holy kind of touch.

Jake undressed her slowly, layer by layer, taking his time like each article of clothing carried weight. Her body trembled beneath his hands — not from nerves, but from the sheer depth of feeling.

She wasn't used to this.
Not the physicality.
But the being seen.

Really seen.

He kissed the swell of her breast, the curve of her waist, the tender space below her navel. Places no one else had lingered. Places that weren't just erogenous — they were intimate.

She lay back against the sheets, breath shallow, limbs warm and loose. Jake hovered above her — strong, grounded, unmoving — like he was covering her in the best sense of the word.

Not claiming.

Not conquering.

But sheltering.

"Tell me what you need," he whispered.

Her voice cracked.

"You. Only you."

And when he entered her, it wasn't sharp.

It wasn't shocking.

It was sacred.

A surrender so complete, her body gave way to it with something like reverence — like it had been waiting for this exact moment, for him, for years.

Every breath she'd ever stifled… every ache she'd buried beneath silence… came undone in the span of a heartbeat.

Her back arched to meet him.

Her lips parted on a gasp that wasn't pain, wasn't pleasure — it was recognition.

Jake moved within her like he knew her. Not just her body, but her grief, her longings, her lonely nights. His hands held her hips firmly, grounding her with every motion. Not to restrain — but to keep her from drifting too far into whatever vast, beautiful place they were now creating together.

His mouth brushed the hollow beneath her ear, the curve of her shoulder, the place where her pulse beat wildly at her temple.

And in return, she clung to him — his back, his hair, his name whispered like a litany, like prayer, like she was anchoring herself to the one thing she trusted not to break.

Tears welled in her eyes before she knew they were coming.

Not from sadness. Not even from joy.

But from something deeper — a collision of grief and hope and the sudden, overwhelming realization that she had been starving, and now she was full.

So full.

Of him.

Of warmth.

Of life.

Of love that hadn't been promised, but had arrived anyway — unannounced, undeniable.

She didn't speak. Didn't need to.

Her body said everything — in the way her legs wrapped tighter around him, in the trembling of her hands against his spine, in the way her breath caught every time he whispered her name like it meant something sacred.

And when she came — it wasn't loud.

It wasn't desperate.

It was a soft, trembling unraveling.

A deep release from the deepest parts of her.

A single exhale, like her soul had finally found room to expand inside her skin.

Her eyes fluttered closed, and his name slipped from her lips again — not shouted, not forced — just... offered.

Like a vow.

Like a beginning.

Like she was finally home. "Jake..."

He held her through it.

Kissed her through it.

Whispered her name like a promise and followed her into that place, shuddering against her skin.

"Thank you," he breathed into her neck.

Later, they lay tangled beneath the blanket. Her head on his chest, his hand resting over her heart.

The room was warm. The silence was full.

"This bed," he said softly, "this room — it's yours. And you let me in. I won't forget that."

Tears pricked her eyes.

"I didn't just bring you in, Jake," she said. "I opened the door and left it wide."

He kissed her forehead, his breath warm against her skin.

"Then I'm never leaving."

She closed her eyes.

And for the first time since Shane died, her body didn't feel like a battlefield.

It felt like home.

Jake kissed her again.

Deeper now.

Not just mouth to mouth — but soul to soul.

His hands explored every curve, every line of her like scripture. Not for possession, but for memory.

He whispered between kisses:

""I want to take care of you," he said softly. And I'll walk through any fire that dares come near you or Dillon."

Rainey blinked, tears welling — and this time, she didn't try to stop them.

Because every word rang true.

This wasn't about forgetting her past.

It was about honoring it.

Carrying it forward — not alone, but with someone willing to walk beside her, even through the flames.

"This," he said, his voice thick with emotion, "this is what love feels like."

And she broke.

Not because it hurt.

But because it didn't.

Because nothing in her body was bracing anymore.
Because she wasn't shrinking or surviving.
Because for the first time in years, she felt safe.

Not only in his arms — but in herself.

Later, curled against his chest, their bodies still joined in the quiet, she whispered:

"I can't lose you."

Jake pressed a kiss to her temple.

"I'm not going anywhere."

She nodded slowly, her voice barely audible.

"Good. Because I already wouldn't know how to live without you."

And he just held her closer.

Not as a possession.

But as a promise.

Chapter Twenty-Two

THE CALM

She woke again before the sun touched the windows.
Not to the panic of a nightmare.
Not to the silence of grief.
But to Jake.

His body was warm against hers, steady and real. One arm rested over her waist, the other draped behind her, anchoring her in place. The weight of him, the closeness — it should've felt unfamiliar. But it didn't.

It felt like the way things should be.

Like something inside her had been waiting for this kind of nearness — not just physically, but spiritually. Someone beside her who asked for nothing and gave everything just by being there.

She kept her eyes closed, breathing in the scent of him — warm skin, faint soap, a whisper of woodsmoke clinging to his hair from the night before. He smelled like comfort. Like grounding.

The world was quiet. Not heavy like it had been most mornings since Shane's death. Not brittle with sorrow or padded in numbness. But quiet in a peaceful way — as if the house itself was taking its first full breath in years.

She thought about how many mornings she'd woken up alone, feeling like a stranger in her own skin. How often she'd reached across the bed instinctively, only to find the hollow space beside her — cold, empty, unforgiving.

But this morning wasn't hollow.

It was full.
Of presence. Of heat. Of breath. Of life.

Tears pooled unexpectedly in her eyes — not from sadness, but from the terrifying realization that she could actually be happy again. And that happiness, no matter how soft or quiet, made her feel disloyal to the past.

But Shane would want this.
She felt it in her bones.

He would want her to breathe. To feel. To wake up with someone kind and strong.
Someone who looked at her like she mattered — not because she was perfect, but because she was his.

Jake stirred behind her, tightening his arm around her waist. He pressed a soft kiss to her bare shoulder.
"You awake?" he murmured, still half-dreaming.
"Yeah," she whispered.
He drew her closer. "You okay?"
She smiled into the pillow. "Better than okay."

There was a pause, just long enough to feel the emotion settle into the space between them.
"Me too," he said, so quietly it barely reached her ears.

They stayed in bed longer than they should have.
Neither of them in a rush to break the spell.

Rainey rolled onto her back and studied him. Jake lay beside her with one arm behind his head, eyes closed, lips parted slightly. The morning light, pale and golden, filtered in through the sheer curtains and carved soft shadows across his chest — over healed scars, ridged muscles, stories she still didn't know.

She reached out and lightly traced a line along his ribs, letting her fingers map him like Braille.

He opened his eyes slowly, looking at her with a calm curiosity. "What're you thinking?" he asked.

She hesitated. "That this is the first time I've woken up and not felt like I was falling."

He nodded, like he understood that kind of gravity.
"And that this house doesn't feel as sad," she added, her voice quieter now.

Jake reached over and tucked a loose strand of hair behind her ear.
"That's not because of me, Rainey. That's because of you."
She tilted her head. "Me?"
"You gave it permission to feel warm again."

She felt the words hit somewhere deep, in a place that had been dormant for far too long. She leaned in and pressed a kiss over his heart.
"I didn't know how much I needed you."
He pulled her into his chest, burying his nose in her hair.
"I think I needed you more."

Later, Rainey padded softly down the hallway in her robe, the floor cool beneath her feet. The house had a rhythm this morning — a hum she hadn't felt in years. Like someone had lifted the veil off a room long shut.

Jake was already in the kitchen, barefoot and bare-chested, moving with quiet purpose. His hands moved over the coffee setup like he'd done it a dozen times before.

He didn't ask where anything was. He didn't fumble.
He just...knew.

"Cream's in the fridge," she said gently, not wanting to startle him.

He opened it without hesitation, poured a splash into her mug, and slid it across the counter.
She picked it up, took a sip, and watched him. "You know exactly how I take it."

He leaned against the counter with his own mug. "I pay attention."
"You do," she said. "You really do. Better than anyone I've ever known."

He met her gaze, steady and quiet. His silence was intimate — a kind of unspoken devotion that didn't need to be performed.

They stood like that for a moment, sipping coffee in the hush of a new day, the silence rich and generous.

She walked to the sink and opened the window slightly. Morning birdsong filtered in, soft and tentative, like the world itself was trying not to interrupt what was forming inside these walls.

Jake stood at the stove, cracking eggs, his presence woven so naturally into the space that it startled her. Not because it was fast — but because it felt right.

"How do you know your way around this kitchen so well?" she asked.

He smiled. "I watched you move through it. Picked up a few things."
"Like what?"
"Where you keep the quiet. Where your favorite mug is. What music you never play anymore."

Rainey blinked. That last one landed. She hadn't touched the old CD player on the shelf since Shane died.
"You notice everything, don't you?"
Jake shrugged. "You notice when you care."

Footsteps echoed down the hallway, slightly uneven and lazy. Dillon appeared in the doorway, hoodie on, hair mussed, mismatched socks.

He stopped short when he saw Jake.
It wasn't tension. It wasn't hesitation.
It was awareness.

Jake nodded. "Morning."
Dillon walked over and kissed his mom on the cheek, then glanced at the coffee cups. "Morning."
"You make extra?" he asked, not quite smirking.
Jake gestured to the counter. "Yours is waiting. Mug with the lightning bolt."
Dillon walked over, picked it up, took a sip.

He made a face. "You put the cinnamon in it?"
Jake lifted a brow. "That's how you took it the other day. Figured it was your thing."
Dillon sipped again. "It's really good, thank you."
Jake smiled and nodded, raising his cup.

Rainey blinked, watching the casual dance between them — this new choreography she didn't expect.

Jake turned back to the stove. "You want eggs?"
Dillon shrugged. "You cooking?"
Jake flipped the spatula in his hand. "I'm trying to earn my keep."
"You're doing okay," Dillon said, sitting down and pulling his hoodie tighter around him.

Rainey leaned on the doorframe, watching the two of them move around each other. Jake handed Dillon a plate, then buttered a piece of toast without being asked. Dillon accepted it with a simple "thanks," and Rainey felt something shift.

This was usually the time of morning where she filled the silence. Where she put on a brave face for her son and tried not to let him see how heavy it all was.

But now... the silence wasn't heavy.
It was natural.
Shared.

After breakfast, Dillon rinsed his plate, and Jake handed him a dishtowel.
"I usually let them drip dry," Dillon said.
Jake smiled and pulled the towel in. "Old habit. Air drying takes too long when you're feeding six kids."

Rainey stiffened slightly. Jake noticed and softened.
"Different chapters," he said quietly. "This one's the one I want to get right."

Dillon glanced at his mom. "We used to play this game," he said suddenly. "After Dad died."
Rainey looked up.
Jake turned to him. "What kind of game?"
Dillon hesitated. "We'd all say one thing we were grateful for. Even

if it was stupid. Like soft socks or pancakes. Just random things you appreciate."

Jake nodded. "That's not stupid. That's sacred."
Dillon cracked a small smile. "You wanna play?"
Jake set the dish down, dried his hands. "I'll go first."

He turned to Rainey.
"I'm grateful for a second chance."
Rainey felt her breath catch.

Jake nodded to Dillon.
"I'm grateful for cinnamon in my coffee."
They both looked at her.

She blinked away the sting in her eyes. "I'm grateful... for this. Everything. Both of you."

Later, after the dishes were done and the house settled into its gentle morning rhythm, Jake pulled her close again, standing just inside the kitchen doorway.

"You okay?" he asked, his voice low.
She nodded. "I'm more than okay."
He cupped her face. "Today was a good day."
"It was a beginning," she said softly. "It was... perfect."

He kissed her — slow, reverent, grounding.

And in that moment, Rainey knew:
This wasn't a temporary peace.
It wasn't a breath held in fear of collapse.
It was a new page.
A new chapter.
The first line of a life that still had love left to write.

Chapter Twenty-Three

THE BITTERSWEET

Rainey

It started with a missed call.

Just a quiet notification on her phone around mid-afternoon — one she nearly ignored. But the name on the screen made her stomach tighten.

Mrs. Carolyn DeMarco.

Shane's mother.

Her thumb hovered over the voicemail icon. She walked slowly into the hallway, away from the soft sounds of Dillon and Jake talking in the kitchen, and pressed play.

"Rainey… it's Carolyn. I, um… I hope you're well. I heard from someone in town — I won't say who — that there's a man staying at the house. I'm not angry. Just surprised. I wish I didn't have to find out this way. I'd really appreciate a call when you get the chance. Okay? That's all. Love you."

The message ended, but Rainey didn't move.

Her heart thudded in her chest. Not from guilt, but something else — something worse.

Fear.

The kind that came with being seen. Judged. Misunderstood.

She sat down slowly on the edge of her bed, phone still in her hand, throat tight.

She hadn't told Carolyn.

Not because she meant to hide Jake — but because she hadn't known how. Because everything between her and Shane had been so deeply honored, so tragically ended, so untouched until now.

Because her grief was still sacred.

And yet here she was, sitting in the same home that once echoed with the rhythm of a love she thought would never end, now pulsing with a new heartbeat, steady and gentle and uninvited by anyone but her.

She ran her hand through her hair, staring at the small framed photo on the dresser. Shane, sunburned and smiling, holding baby Dillon on his shoulders.

Her throat burned.

Jake found her there twenty minutes later.

He knocked softly, then stepped inside.

Rainey didn't look up.

"She called," she said.

Jake moved to her without hesitation and knelt beside the bed.

"Who, sweetheart?"

"Shane's mom." Her eyes stayed on the floor. "She left a message. Someone told her there was a man here."

Jake didn't speak right away. He didn't press her. He just took her hand.

"I wasn't trying to avoid it," Rainey whispered. "I didn't want to keep you secret. I just... I didn't know how to talk about this."

"You don't owe me an explanation."

"I owe her one."

Jake nodded. "Then call her. Let her hear your voice. That's all she really wants."

Rainey's eyes filled, but she didn't cry. "I'm scared she'll think I'm replacing Shane."

Jake's grip tightened gently.

"No one could replace him. And anyone who loved him knows you wouldn't try."

He stood and sat beside her, brushing her hair back from her face.

"You didn't betray anyone, Rainey. You're surviving. And you're doing it with love."

She sat with the phone in her hand for almost an hour before dialing.

When Carolyn answered, her voice was softer than Rainey expected.

"Rainey."

"Hi, Carolyn."

A pause.

"I didn't mean to upset you."

"You didn't. I just... wasn't ready to be found out like that."

"I understand."

Rainey took a breath. "There's a man. His name is Jake. He's staying here. I wasn't hiding him... I just didn't know how to talk about it."

"I understand," Carolyn said again.

"You do?"

"I wasn't surprised because you met someone," Carolyn said gently. "I prayed for that. I was surprised because I assumed you knew. I assumed you knew how much we love you — and that you deserve to be happy."

Tears stung Rainey's eyes. "I didn't want anyone to think I was replacing Shane."

"No one thinks that. No one could ever question your love for Shane. You loved each other deeply, and you lived a beautiful life together for many years."

"I still love him."

"I know you do. What you shared will never die. But loving him doesn't mean you have to be alone, Rainey. You deserve joy. You deserve to smile again, to laugh. You deserve to be loved."

Rainey pressed a hand over her mouth, trembling.

Carolyn's voice softened. "Shane would want that for you. He would want you and Dillon to be loved — and protected."

Through a flood of tears, Rainey whispered, "You don't know what you've given me with this phone call."

Carolyn paused, then said: "Rainey, you've given me the greatest gift a mother can ever receive — you loved, and still love, my son beyond anything I could have hoped for. I will always be grateful to you. And I pray that you and Dillon live a life filled with joy and comfort... every day forward, for the rest of your lives."

Rainey wept quietly, cradling the phone.

"Take your time," Carolyn added. "But don't waste any."

That last part hit hard. **Don't waste the time you're given**.

Jake was waiting on the back porch when she stepped outside, face damp with tears but calm.

He stood as soon as she appeared, crossing the distance in three long strides.

"She was so kind," Rainey said, walking into his arms.

Jake pulled her close. "I hoped she would be."

"She said she prayed I would find someone. That she assumed I knew they'd still love me — even if I found someone else."

Jake's hand ran gently up and down her spine. "They're good people."

"She said Shane would want me to be protected."

Jake kissed her temple. "Of course he wants that. I intend to honor him and his legacy."

Rainey closed her eyes, pressing her face to his chest.

"He'd like you."

Jake smiled into her hair. "Then I won't let either of you down."

That night, as they sat on the couch after Dillon went to bed, Rainey curled into Jake's side, their fingers laced.

She didn't say anything at first. She just listened to the quiet. To the soft ticking of the clock. To the echo of Carolyn's words in her mind.

"I feel like something broke open today," she said softly.

Jake looked down at her. "Does it hurt?"

"No," she whispered. "It feels like healing."

He rested his cheek on her head. "Then it's about time."

They sat like that for a long while, unmoving.

Because for the first time in years, Rainey wasn't afraid of what came next.

She was ready to live it.

Chapter Twenty-Four

THE UNDERTOW

Jake

It started with a knock on the doorframe.

Not loud. Not hesitant. Just… there. A presence.

Jake looked up from the book he wasn't really reading. The words had long since blurred together. He'd been holding the page open for fifteen minutes, eyes drifting but mind stuck on everything that wasn't on the page.

Dillon stood at the edge of the hallway, hoodie sleeves pushed halfway up, one hand gripping the side of the frame, the other dangling at his side.

"Hey," Dillon said.

Jake straightened in the armchair. "Hey."

"You busy?"

Jake shut the book and set it aside. "Nope."

Dillon walked in slowly, not shy, but not rushed either. There was a kind of weight to the way he moved — not physical, but emotional. Like whatever he was carrying had aged him just a little, made him older than his years.

He sat across from Jake in the other armchair — the one Rainey had once called the "lonely chair" because no one ever used it. Legs tucked beneath him, he looked smaller somehow, like a kid again. But his eyes... his eyes were steady.

"Can I ask you something?" Dillon said.

Jake nodded. "Anything."

A beat. Then:

"Did you ever want to leave?"

Jake's brows lifted slightly. "Leave?"

Dillon looked down, then back up. "Like... your job. Your kids. Your life. Just walk away from it all."

Jake let the silence settle. He didn't rush the answer. This wasn't a casual question.

He leaned forward, elbows on his knees, fingers clasped loosely.

"Yeah," he said. "A few times."

Dillon didn't flinch. He looked like he expected that.

"But I never did," Jake added. "Even when it hurt. Even when I felt like staying was killing something inside me."

"Why?"

Jake looked past him for a second, like the answer was somewhere on the wall behind the boy. Then he brought his eyes back to Dillon's.

"Because I couldn't stand the idea of someone I loved waking up and thinking I gave up on them."

Dillon's mouth twitched, like he wanted to smile but didn't quite trust it.

Jake leaned back, letting the words breathe. "Sometimes I still looked like I wasn't there," he admitted. "Distance does that. Work schedules. Complicated adults. Courts. Bitterness. But I didn't stop loving my kids. Not for a second."

Dillon nodded, slow and thoughtful. "People always say love means staying. But sometimes people stay and still feel gone."

Jake exhaled. "Yeah. You're right."

"And sometimes people leave," Dillon added quietly, "without meaning to."

That was it.

That was the heart of it.

Jake knew now — this wasn't about him.

This was about Shane.

About a fourteen-year-old boy who had watched his father die on a hotel floor and had spent the last two years trying to make sense of that moment — not just with pain, but with meaning.

And somehow, grief had sculpted Dillon into someone wise. Not hardened, not angry — just aware.

Jake nodded slowly. "You're carrying a lot, Dillon."

"I'm okay," he said with a shrug. "I got good at not dropping stuff."

Jake smiled, sad and proud all at once.

"Can I tell you something?" Jake asked.

Dillon looked up. "Sure."

Jake's voice was quieter now. "Your mom talks about your dad like he was a saint. And honestly? The way she looks at you... there's not a doubt in my mind he left behind the best part of himself."

Dillon blinked, but didn't interrupt.

Jake went on, "You've got this strength in you. Not loud. Not showy. But solid. You protect her without saying it. I see it."

Dillon looked down at his hands.

"You don't need another father," Jake said gently. "You had a great one. And you're definitely not a kid anymore. But if you ever want someone in your corner — someone who shows up and doesn't flinch — I'm here. No expectations. No replacing anyone. Just... here."

Dillon didn't speak at first.

But something in his posture eased.

Like he'd been holding a door halfway shut, and now it had creaked open a few inches.

Then, casually:

"I'm building a new computer next week. You any good with tools?"

Jake smiled. "I'm good with whatever you need."

Rainey

She watched from the hallway.

Neither of them saw her.

She'd come to ask Jake if he wanted coffee. Something mundane. Something simple. But she'd stopped cold when she heard Dillon's voice. And then Jake's.

It had taken everything in her not to step into the room. Not to fold herself into Jake's arms. Not to weep.

Because what she heard wasn't just vulnerability. It was acceptance.

She had worried for months about how this moment would happen — the conversation, the reckoning, the unspoken fears between a grieving son and the man who might one day become part of their story.

But it didn't feel like a reckoning.

It felt like... peace.

Jake hadn't tried to win him over. He hadn't talked down to him or tried to fix anything. He had listened. Offered space. Gave him truth.

And Dillon — God, her boy — he hadn't bristled or shut down. He had spoken like a man. A young one, yes, but a man whose grief had not made him bitter. It only added to the resilience and the remarkableness of the person he was before.

She saw Shane in him.

The methodic. The integrity. The sensibility. The ambition.

But she also saw herself.

The softness. The courage. The sensitivity. The determination.

And now, somehow, she saw Jake there too — not as an invader or a replacement, but as a man slowly being welcomed.

This wasn't about passion anymore. It wasn't about protection.

It wasn't even about healing.

This was about belonging.

And for the first time since Shane died, Rainey didn't feel like she was waiting for something to be taken away.

She felt — down to the center of her soul — that something had finally been given.

Jake

Jake glanced toward the window. The sky outside was streaked with the late-morning light, soft and silver-blue. Somewhere in the house, a floorboard creaked — Rainey, probably, moving through the kitchen or pausing by the stairs.

He could feel her.

Not just physically, but emotionally.

Jake turned back to Dillon. "What are you building in the system? Gaming rig?"

Dillon nodded. "Yeah. Dual monitor setup. Water-cooled CPU. I've been saving up."

Jake whistled. "Nice. You do all that yourself?"

"Most of it. My dad helped me build my first one."

Jake nodded with respect. "He taught you well."

"Yeah," Dillon said. Then, after a breath: "He'd like you."

Jake felt something knot in his throat.

He cleared it, trying not to let the emotion sit too long.

"I hope so," he said.

"You're not trying too hard," Dillon added. "That's probably why."

Jake grinned. "Trying too hard's never been my thing."

Dillon stood up, stretching.

"You wanna help me plan the build? I have parts coming Monday."

Jake rose to his feet. "Absolutely."

Dillon walked ahead, and Jake followed — quiet, steady, grateful.

Rainey

Rainey stepped into the hallway as they passed. She didn't say a word.

Dillon glanced at her and gave a nod that said everything. Not permission. Not approval. Just peace.

And Jake — he didn't stop to kiss her or say something poetic.

He just reached out as he passed, brushed his hand along hers, fingers warm, calloused, certain.

And that was enough.

Because in that quiet hallway, with no grand declarations or choreographed grace, Rainey finally understood:

This wasn't the aftermath of love.

It wasn't survival.

It was life.

And it had chosen them, not the other way around.

Chapter Twenty-Five

THE TIDE

Rainey

She noticed it first in the way he didn't meet her eyes.

It was just after breakfast. Dillon had gone outside to ride his bike — the air cool and crisp, tinged with the first blush of fall. Rainey stood by the sink, rinsing dishes, while Jake lingered near the window, nursing his coffee with a stillness that didn't match the morning.

He had his phone in hand. Face lit by the screen. Brow low.

Not smiling. Not talking. Just… gone.

Not physically.

But pulled inward — like someone hearing a sound only they could hear. Like someone already halfway out the door without moving a muscle.

She dried her hands and approached quietly, trying not to break the moment. "Everything okay?"

Jake didn't look up.

He just nodded, eyes still locked on the screen. "Work."

That one word fell between them like a stone, cracking the warmth they'd built over the past few days.

Work.

He never brought it into the house. Not really. He talked in abstractions — vague mentions of flights or late nights. But he never shared the tension. Never vented. Never answered calls during dinner or carried the cold edge of a briefing into their mornings.

Until now.

Rainey watched him closely. His jaw was tight, thumb frozen mid-scroll. His shoulders weren't relaxed like usual — they were drawn inward, like he was bracing for something.

And just like that, she was afraid.

Not of what he'd say. But of what he wouldn't.

He didn't talk much that afternoon.

Rainey gave him space. Not because she was calm — but because she was scared.

Scared that if she asked too many questions, he'd retreat even further. Scared that the man who once held her like she was oxygen would begin to disappear — not in a rush, but in that slow, terrifying way that grief had already taught her: one breath, one heartbeat, one moment too late.

She folded laundry in silence. Scrubbed out a drawer she hadn't touched in a year. Reorganized the pantry just to feel like something made sense.

All the while, Jake moved like a ghost through the house.

Pacing. Checking his phone. Walking outside and coming back in. Taking a call near the back door with a voice too low to hear.

By dinnertime, she'd counted fewer than ten words from him.

When Dillon asked, "Hey Jake, you okay?"

Jake gave a tired half-smile that didn't reach his eyes and said, "Long day."

That was it.

Rainey didn't sleep that night.

Even with Jake lying beside her.

Even with his hand on her waist.

Because something inside him was locked tight.

And she didn't know how to find the key.

Jake

He knew he was slipping.

Not away from her.

But back into himself — the version of him he kept buried under quiet mornings and soft kisses and whispered promises that maybe, just maybe, this was finally a life he could live.

But the call that morning had shattered the illusion.

It was a name.

A case.

A set of coordinates he thought were buried for good.

Suddenly, he was back in a hotel hallway in Prague, tracing blood from a shattered suitcase. Back in the cargo hold of a C-17, watching customs officials unzip a duffel bag they would never forget. Back inside a debriefing room where the words "child trafficking" and "high-value target" weren't just headlines — they were faces burned into his memory.

He wasn't slipping because he didn't love her.

He was slipping because he didn't know how to bring that part of himself into her world.

This wasn't a man who forgot to take the trash out.

This was a man who still dreamed about the sound a nine-millimeter makes when it hits flesh at close range.

And now, he stood in her kitchen, watching her butter toast and hum to the rhythm of a quiet morning, and he felt like a damn liar.

He didn't know how to say it.

Didn't know how to explain that just hearing the name again had triggered a kind of mental vertigo.

And so he didn't say anything at all.

He watched her walk softly, like she didn't want to spook him.

And it broke his heart.

Because she'd lived through this before — not with him, but with absence.

And silence, to someone like Rainey, wasn't a blank page.

It was a countdown.

That night, as she lay beside him, her back to his chest, he felt the distance grow wider with every breath.

She wasn't asleep.

He knew the rhythm of her sleep by now — the little exhale she made when she dropped into it. The twitch of her fingers.

But tonight, she was perfectly still.

Still in that way that said: I don't want to make this worse.

Jake reached out and placed his hand on her hip.

Just to feel her.

Just to anchor himself to something real.

She reached back, found his hand, wrapped her fingers around it.

But she didn't turn.

Didn't speak.

And he understood why.

Because when someone has lived through sudden loss, silence feels like the first symptom of goodbye.

And he hated himself for making her feel that again.

He stared at the ceiling long after he believed she had fallen asleep — breath finally soft, hand still in his.

And for the first time in a long time, Jake felt afraid.

Not of the job. Not of the case.

But of ruining this.

This quiet, sacred thing they'd built.

He didn't know how to tell her that he felt split in half. That the man who held her so gently was the same man who once kicked down doors with a weapon drawn. That there were pieces of his past that didn't have tidy endings — only blood and compromise.

He worried that if she knew everything, she would see him differently. Not as strong. Not as safe.

But broken.

And maybe too broken to be trusted with something as whole as her.

But what he didn't know — what he couldn't yet feel — was that Rainey wasn't slipping away.

She was staying.

She had been through the worst already. And this? This was still human. Still recoverable. Still love.

In the dark, she whispered so softly he almost missed it:

"Whatever it is... you can tell me when you're ready."

Jake's eyes burned. He tightened his grip on her hand.

And for the first time that day, he breathed.

Not because everything was resolved — but because even silence, when it's wrapped in love, can become a place to rest.

Maybe that was enough.

At least for now.

Or maybe... it was only the beginning.

Chapter Twenty-Six

SUBMISSION

Rainey

She still wasn't asleep. She hadn't slept at all.

Jake lay behind her — close, warm, steady.

But his breath? Too controlled. Too even. Like a man trying hard not to shatter. Like someone fighting to stay present in a body that wanted to disappear.

The space between them wasn't wide.

But it was loud — thick with everything unsaid, everything they both carried.

And then... he moved.

Not with urgency.

But with intention — slow, measured, unmistakably clear.

His hand slid up slowly, finding her waist, then her ribs. He shifted closer, his chest pressing into her back, the weight of him settling behind her like armor. His rigidity masterful. Intentional. Contained.

His breath touched her ear. Still, he didn't speak.

His palm moved higher, between her breasts. Up the center of her chest. Over the hollow of her throat.

And stayed there.

Her heart pounded beneath his fingers.

She didn't move. She didn't resist.

He was in pain. And somehow, she knew this — this — was how he needed to feel tethered again.

She whispered, "Jake?"

Still, he said nothing.

But his hand—firm, steady—tightened just slightly. Not enough to choke. Just enough to hold.

The air caught between her lips. Not in fear. But in awe. And maybe a little fear, too.

She'd never done this before. Never let someone touch her like this. Never let someone take her this far from herself just to bring her back.

His hand didn't move. But his body shifted—closer, heavier, his breath warmer now.

Then came the voice. Low. Controlled. Quiet.

"Touch yourself."

Her eyes fluttered closed. She didn't answer. Couldn't.

"I said," he repeated, slower, more precise, "touch yourself."

Her hand slid down her stomach, trembling.

This wasn't about arousal. Not only.

This was about trust. About letting herself be seen while she was afraid, unsure—and still choosing to do it anyway.

Jake's hand on her throat stayed firm. Not cruel. Not violent. Grounding. Commanding.

"I've never..." she whispered.

"Shhhh... I know," he murmured. "Don't speak."

Her fingers found the heat between her thighs. She gasped softly.

Jake's grip remained, his mouth brushing the shell of her ear.

"That's it."

A tremble ran through her.

His breath came faster now, though his body stayed still.

"You're going to come like this," he whispered, "with my hand on your throat and your fingers doing what I tell you."

She arched slightly into him, needing more—more contact, more closeness, more him. She felt his hardness throbbing in rhythm against her bowed back.

"You're mine," he said, voice deepening. "Do you understand me?"

"Yes," she breathed.

"Say it."

"I'm yours."

"Such a beautiful woman. You unravel me."

Her hand moved lower, fingers slipping beneath the softness of her sleep shorts, tentative and trembling.

Jake stayed still behind her—anchoring her, commanding her without moving, without even needing to.

His hand on her throat was both weight and invitation. Not pressure. Just presence.

"Slower," he murmured. "Feel everything."

Her breath caught.

She was already wet. Already aching. Not because she needed release, but because she was his.

His.

Her fingers circled softly, experimentally, and Jake's fingers flexed just slightly against her skin in approval.

She moaned—quietly, unsure if she was allowed.

He pressed his mouth to her ear. "Don't hold it in. Give me every sound."

And so she did.

It wasn't polished or practiced. It wasn't how she'd imagined it in a younger life when shame and modesty kept her locked in a body she'd never explored.

It was raw. Real.

She began to move in rhythm with her own hand—small gasps escaping her lips. Her body arched slightly into him, needing more, needing him closer even as he held her still.

Jake's other hand gripped her waist now, grounding her, his breath harsh against the back of her neck.

"That's it," he whispered. "You're doing so good."

The praise wrecked her.

It unraveled something buried.

And as the waves built, as her thighs trembled and her breath fractured into pieces, she cried out—not just from pleasure, but from the release of being seen.

She shattered around her own hand, her body writhing, Jake's hand firm at her throat, his voice low and certain.

"Yes," he growled. "So beautiful. You're all I've ever needed."

She lay there, shaking, still half-clothed and undone in the most intimate way she'd ever known.

Jake kissed her shoulder, her neck, her temple, slowly sliding his mouth down to her nipples. Then lower. He tasted her, cleaning every inch of her before speaking another word.

Then he moved her hand aside and took her face in both of his.

"Look at me," he said.

Her eyes fluttered open.

She was vulnerable, wide open—but not afraid.

"I needed that," he said, his voice thick with something rough and unspoken.

"I know."

"You make me glad to be alive," he said. "Do you know that?"

Rainey nodded. "I do."

He kissed her then—deep, slow, filled with emotion that had no name.

And for the first time in hours, he wasn't distant. He was home.

They lay tangled together, skin to skin, her head against his chest, his arms tight around her as if afraid she'd slip through.

Rainey reached up, running her fingertips along the stubble on his jaw.

"Talk to me," she whispered.

Jake sighed, the kind of sound that comes from the soul. "It's a case I thought was closed. Years ago. But this morning... it came back."

She didn't ask for details. She didn't need to.

"What do you need?" she asked.

He pressed his forehead to hers. "I need to know this doesn't break what we're building."

Rainey's answer was immediate. "Then don't carry it alone."

Jake nodded, barely. "I've never had this. A place to land. A reason to come home. You and Dillon... you're the only thing that's ever made me want to stay still."

"You don't have to stay still," she whispered. "You just have to stay honest."

His eyes glistened. "I will. I swear to you, Rainey. No more silence."

She leaned up and kissed him, slow and fierce.

And when they finally drifted into sleep that night, it wasn't just as lovers tangled in shared desire.

It was as something more — something unspoken but deeply understood.

As partners. As soul-bound survivors of everything life had tried to take from them.

Two hearts choosing, again and again, to stay — not because it was easy, but because the ache of healing was worth it.

Together.

Always, together.

Chapter Twenty-Seven

THE GRAVITY

Jake

The call came just after 9 a.m.

Rainey was in the shower, steam curling beneath the bathroom door. Dillon was still upstairs, working on a history project he had spread across the entire desk like a miniature war room. The house was calm, lit with that soft, filtered light that only came from overcast skies in early autumn. The kind of light that made everything feel suspended—timeless, safe.

Jake was in the kitchen, standing barefoot in front of the window, cradling a half-empty mug. His thumb traced the rim of the ceramic absentmindedly, the coffee inside long since cooled. The smell of rain hung in the air, faint but electric, and in that stillness, his phone buzzed against the counter.

Unknown number. Washington area code.

He stared at it. Not just a glance. A full, weighted pause.

Then he picked up. Instinct. Muscle memory. That coiled part of him that never fully relaxed.

"Yeah."

The voice on the other end was clipped. Familiar.

"Jake. It's Monroe. You got a minute?"

Jake closed his eyes, jaw flexing. The taste of old adrenaline seemed to coat his tongue. "What is it?"

Monroe never wasted time. He didn't ask how you were. Didn't bullshit. Didn't soften things.

"There's movement on the Santiago case. The Bureau's pulling older assets for briefing debriefs — former transport marshals, intel leads, security officers. You're flagged."

Jake didn't speak.

"Not asking you to come in. Not yet," Monroe continued. "Just letting you know they'll push. You're still in the system."

Jake's hand curled tighter around the mug. His knuckles turned white.

"I'm not available."

"I figured. But it's not up to me. You still have clearance. They'll try to loop you in."

Jake glanced down the hallway. The water was still running. The sound of Rainey's soft humming bled faintly through the walls.

"I'm not who I was," he said quietly.

"No," Monroe said. "But they don't care about that."

The line went dead.

Rainey

When she stepped out of the bathroom, towel wrapped tightly at her chest, the mirrors fogged and her skin still flushed from the heat, she found Jake fully dressed.

Boots laced. Shirt tucked. Shoulder holster lying on the counter beside his phone like a ghost from a life she thought he'd left behind.

He didn't see her at first. He was standing near the fridge, unmoving. Tense.

The fridge's hum was the only sound in the room.

"Where are you going?" she asked carefully, her voice breaking the quiet like a dropped dish.

Jake turned slowly. His face was hard to read. He'd been quiet lately, but this wasn't quiet. This was armored. His eyes were shadowed—guarded in a way they hadn't been in weeks.

"Nowhere," he said. "Just thinking."

She stepped closer, toes curling into the cool tile floor. The air between them felt different this morning. Tighter. Heavier.

"About what?"

"Work."

That word again.

She hated it now. Not because of what it meant. But because of what it didn't.

They ate breakfast quietly.

Dillon came downstairs, grabbed a protein bar, and headed back up with a mumbled "thanks." Jake nodded but said little. He was polite. Present in body, but not in mind.

Not like last night. Not like the hours after she'd surrendered everything — her body, her trust, the last fragile pieces of fear she'd carried since Shane.

Now his jaw was tight. His gaze didn't linger. He sipped his coffee mechanically, as if it were fuel rather than comfort.

And Rainey felt it.

Not fear. Not yet. Something more dangerous: disconnection.

She pushed scrambled eggs around her plate but didn't eat. The air felt dense. Like before a storm. Like something unsaid was pressing on the walls of the house.

She studied him—the way he sat, spine rigid, eyes on a fixed point that didn't exist.

It reminded her of Shane, once. A week before he died. He'd been silent for two days. She'd asked what was wrong, and he'd said, "Nothing. Just tired." And then... he was gone.

Her fingers twitched against the fork.

She couldn't go through that again.

He rinsed his plate and set it in the sink with too much care.

Something about the silence cracked her.

"Did something happen?" she asked.

Jake nodded once. "Got a call."

"From who?"

"Someone I used to work with. They're trying to reactivate old personnel. It's not urgent."

"But it's enough to shift the air in this house."

Jake turned to her slowly, brow drawn.

"I told him I'm not available."

She crossed her arms. "Are you?"

His mouth opened — then closed again.

"Yes," he said finally. "To you. To Dillon. To this."

"Then tell your face."

The words came out sharper than she meant.

Jake looked at her like she'd struck him — not in pain, but recognition.

She didn't back down. "You don't get to disappear and then tell me you're still here."

"I'm not disappearing," he said. "I'm bracing."

"For what?"

"For whatever part of my past decides to crawl back out."

Jake

He wanted to reach for her. Wanted to explain.

But something inside him resisted. That old voice. The one that said, Keep your edge. Stay silent. Don't expose weakness.

But this wasn't the job. This was her.

And she was staring at him now — the woman who had laid her entire life in his hands — and Jake saw it:

Not anger. Not disappointment. But fear.

The kind that comes from having already lost once before.

She didn't think he would hurt her.

She thought he would quietly vanish. Inch by inch. Like Shane.

Jake swallowed hard. "There are parts of my past I've tried to lock away. But the second that call came in... they were all standing in the room again."

"Do you want to go back?" she asked.

"No....God, no."

Then softer, "I want to want to stay. I do."

"Then what's stopping you?"

He didn't answer. Not immediately.

Because it wasn't just the call. It wasn't just Monroe.

It was the flash of a memory from the night before — the way Rainey had laughed when she picked up a call from her friend Natalie. The way her voice changed, playful and light. The way she smiled while talking about the gallery reopening downtown.

Jake had felt it then — sharp, irrational, and harder to admit than anger.

Jealousy.

Not of a man. Not even of a specific memory.

But of a life he hadn't been part of.

Of the version of her that had once belonged to someone else — to another rhythm, another world he couldn't touch. And worse, the fear that some small part of her might still miss it.

He saw it sometimes when her silence stretched too long in the evenings.

When her eyes lingered on old photos, her thumb grazing across faces he'd never met.

When she slipped into that distant look — the one that told him she'd gone somewhere he couldn't follow.

And sometimes, it was simpler than that.

Sometimes it was just *her*.

The way her hips moved across the room without trying.

The effortless grace in the way she tucked her hair, or the soft curve of her mouth when she didn't know he was watching.

She was beautiful — not the kind of beauty that faded or asked for attention, but the kind that commanded it. The kind men remembered. Desired. Maybe even tried to claim.

And it scared the hell out of him.

Because Jake didn't just want her beside him.

He wanted to be enough — for her present, her pain, her joy, her hunger.

He wanted to be the reason she no longer looked back.Because Jake didn't know if he could ever be that man — the one who fit into the elegant, graceful world Rainey came from.

He was boots and blood and battlefields.

And she was art and warmth and candlelight.

Rainey stepped closer, but slowly. Like she sensed something was breaking open and didn't want to spook it.

"Jake," she said. "Whatever this is, we can face it. But I need you to tell me what's happening in your head."

He dragged his hands down his face.

"You want to know what's happening in my head?" he asked. "I'm standing in this kitchen thinking about how one phone call can pull me back into a life that nearly destroyed me — and how that same life could cost me this."

"This?" she echoed.

"You."

He looked down. "You and Dillon and mornings that don't start with threat assessments."

Rainey's face softened.

Jake continued. "And there's a part of me that's terrified I don't deserve any of it. That you'll wake up and realize I'm not enough. That what I carry will eventually weigh this house down."

She shook her head. "You think I don't carry weight too?"

"Yours is beautiful," he said. "It made you kinder. Mine made me harder."

"No," she whispered. "Yours made you fight."

He stepped toward her, then hesitated. "What if I don't know how to stop fighting? What if this life with you — this peace — feels more like a mission I'm not equipped for?"

Rainey reached for him.

But before she could touch his face, Jake took her hand and placed it against his chest.

"Feel that?" he said.

His heart was pounding.

"I'm not afraid of dying," he said. "I'm afraid of losing this. And I don't even know if I have a right to call it mine yet."

"You do," she said.

He shook his head. "I want to protect you from all the things I've seen. But sometimes I think I'm the one you need protecting from."

Rainey didn't pull away.

"You don't need to protect me, Jake. You need to let me in."

She stepped closer and wrapped her arms around his waist, her cheek against his chest.

Jake held her. Hard. Desperate.

"I'm not leaving," he said.

"Then stop holding your breath."

He nodded against her hair. "I want this life. I just... I've never been taught how to have it."

Rainey leaned back and cupped his face.

"Then I'll *teach* you."

He kissed her then — not with hunger, but with relief. A kiss that said thank you, and I'm sorry, and don't give up on me yet.

And for the first time since the call, Jake let himself believe this could last.

That he could last.

And somewhere upstairs, Dillon's laughter floated faintly through the vents — a soft, innocent sound that reminded Jake what this life could be if he stayed.

Really stayed.

Chapter Twenty-Eight

THE RECKONING

Dillon

Jake didn't knock. He just leaned against the doorframe and waited.

Dillon looked up from the circuit board spread across his desk, screwdriver in one hand, a half-melted soldering port under inspection. He squinted behind his glasses. "What's up?"

Jake nodded toward the soldering iron. "That new?"

"Borrowed it from my science teacher," Dillon said. "I have a robotics presentation due Monday. Wiring's trash, though. School gave us a bunch of junk parts."

Jake stepped further into the room, careful — not in a stiff way, but in a way that said he respected the space. As if everything in the room was a page from someone else's life and he didn't want to smudge the ink.

"You mind if I watch?"

Dillon hesitated. Not because he didn't want him there — he just wasn't sure what it would feel like. Sharing this space. This version of himself.

"Sure," he said finally. "Just don't breathe too hard. I'm trying not to fry this port."

Jake smiled. "Got it."

He folded his arms and leaned back against the far wall, watching in silence as Dillon hovered over the tiny board, tweezers in one hand, micro wire in the other.

For a few minutes, there was nothing but the faint sound of clicking and the occasional quiet exhale. Dillon worked with the precision of someone who wasn't just trying to finish — he was trying to get it right. Jake could see that. And something about that moved him.

Jake had seen a lot of things in his life. Firefights. Briefings. Foreign cities lit up by warning flares. But there was something uniquely powerful about watching a boy try to bring a fragile little machine to life with steady hands and borrowed tools.

"Can I ask you something?" Dillon said, eyes still locked on the board.

"Anything."

"Do you ever feel like when things are finally good... that's when you should worry?"

Jake paused.

Dillon glanced at him, but not directly. He kept his hands steady. "I mean, isn't that usually when life messes it all up?" he asked. "Like... the second you let your guard down, that's when everything breaks again?"

Jake let out a slow breath. "Yeah," he said. "That's exactly when."

Dillon didn't answer right away. He just let the quiet sit.

"So what do you do?" he asked.

Jake stepped forward, closer, but not too close. "You do it anyway."

Dillon's brow furrowed. "You mean you take the risk?"

Jake nodded. "You let things be good. Even if they might break. Especially if they might break."

Dillon sat back slightly. "Sounds reckless."

"It's brave," Jake said.

They both smiled a little. And Dillon didn't say it out loud, but something settled in his chest. Because Jake didn't try to fix the question. Didn't try to steer him away from the fear. He just stood in it with him — unflinching. He showed up.

"I used to think," Dillon said after a moment, "that my dad dying was my fault."

Jake's face changed — just slightly. He didn't speak, but he leaned forward a little.

"Yeah, I know it's not logical," Dillon went on. "That's why I've never even said anything. But I'm the reason we went on that trip when we did. I begged him to take us. He wanted to wait a while longer because we had just moved and he had a lot of stuff going on with work and everything."

Jake's jaw tightened.

"He only did it because I wouldn't shut up about it. I probably made him feel guilty because I reminded him how I'd just started a new school and he promised we'd have all these adventures."

Jake stepped forward and crouched near the chair, his voice low. "Dillon, that wasn't your fault."

Dillon nodded. "I know that now. Mostly. But for a while, I thought I broke something. Like I asked for something, and it cost me everything." He paused, "And...my mom. "

They'd just returned to the hotel from a day filled with shopping, street vendors and laughter, followed by an outdoor dinner overlooking Lake Pontchartrain. Dillon was proudly taking practice swings with the new golf club his uncle had given him, as Rainey watched from the couch and Shane beamed close by, casually cautioning him about the overhead chandelier. Shane stepped into the bedroom to plug in his phone. Dillon ran to the bathroom, humming, hands already lathered at the sink.

A sound — jagged, guttural — tore through the air like a rip in reality.

Screaming.

At first, it didn't sound human. Didn't sound like his mother. Too wild. Too broken. But something in his chest knew.

He froze.

The scream came again — louder, more desperate — and instinct shoved him toward the sound.

He rounded the corner and his world collapsed.

Shane - on the floor. Unmoving. Eyes wide and blank. Mouth slightly parted. The kind of stillness that didn't belong to sleep.

And Rainey — God, his mother — bent over him, sobbing, her hands slamming down against his chest again and again. Her voice cracking as she screamed his name, pleaded with a God that didn't seem to be listening, begged her husband to come back, to breathe, to please, just breathe.

She yelled for Dillon to call 911, but her voice was nearly swallowed by the chaos in his own head. The sound of her panic, the slap of her palms against Shane's chest, the rush of merciless terror surging through his whole body — one endless scream.

Jake wanted to tell him no child should carry that. But he didn't rush in.

Dillon looked at the soldering board again. "That's probably why I like stuff like this. You mess up a connection, you can fix it. There's a path. A process. It doesn't vanish. It doesn't pretty much obliterate everything else."

Jake swallowed hard. "That's a lot to carry."

Dillon shrugged. "It's okay. I just never imagined…it could happen to us. He'd be gone."

Jake scanned the shelves — small cluttered things: books about logic gates, a box of old LEGO figures, framed snapshots of Dillon and Shane in matching baseball caps. One photo had Shane laughing with his eyes shut while Dillon — maybe seven at the time — grinned through a mouthful of ice cream.

Jake pointed to it. "You remember that day?"

Dillon nodded. "We were in Santa Fe. I'd just lost my first tooth on the drive there."

Jake smiled and leaned in on the photo. "He looks like a good man. A great dad."

"He was," Dillon said. "We did a lot together. Fishing. Hunting. Pranking mom."

Jake laughed quietly.

"He was really smart, too." Dillon added. "I miss him."

Jake felt something tighten in his chest.

"I wish I could've known him," he said.

Dillon didn't say anything for a while. Then: "I think he would've liked you."

That hit Jake harder than anything had in weeks.

Jake walked slowly to the desk and sat on the edge, keeping a respectful distance. "You know," he said, "I think he's very proud of you. The way you've taken care of your mom. The way you've protected her. And look at you – doing all of these amazing things. It's pretty clear you're a solid reflection of him."

Dillon smiled, tears in his eyes, but too strong to cry.

They didn't hug. Didn't need to. The silence between them wasn't heavy anymore. It was solid. Earned. And now – more than ever before – Jake knew they **needed** and *deserved* someone capable of carrying them through all the storms before...and those to come.

Rainey

She found Jake in the laundry room that evening, folding towels with the precision of a man trying to control something.

She stood in the doorway, watching. His movements were stiff, careful — like folding cloth might hold the world together.

"You don't have to do that," she said softly.

"I know."

He didn't look up.

Rainey stepped forward and laid her hand over his.

"Talk to me."

Jake stilled.

Then slowly turned toward her, every breath in his chest full of something old and unspoken.

"I don't know how to do this part," he said.

"What part?"

He looked at her like the words were foreign. "The staying. The… letting me be enough."

Rainey blinked back a wave of emotion. "You are enough."

Jake lowered his head until his forehead rested against hers.

"I just keep waiting for someone to take it away," he whispered. "For you to wake up and realize I'm still full of too many locked doors."

"I've seen inside them," she said softly. "And I'm still here."

Jake didn't move. He didn't need to. Because in that moment, Rainey felt it — the shift. The breath. The surrender.

He wasn't holding on out of fear anymore. He was staying out of faith.

They didn't make love that night.
They didn't need to.

They lay together in bed — her head on his chest, his hand in her hair — the silence between them no longer heavy, just *honest*.

They didn't talk about the call that morning.
Or the past he was afraid might follow him in.
Or the future they still weren't sure how to name.

Instead, Jake whispered, "I love you."

And Rainey melted.

She'd felt it long before he said it — in his hands, his steadiness, his quiet grief. But hearing it now cracked something open.

She didn't say it back like an echo.
She said it like an answer.

"I love you, Jake Walker."

Jake

He stood outside on the porch just past midnight, cool air brushing his skin, the sky black and endless above him.

The stars were faint tonight. Fewer than usual. But still there.

He heard the door creak behind him. Soft footsteps.
Dillon.

The boy stepped up beside him, hoodie pulled tight, hands buried in his pockets.
"It's nice out here," he said. "You come out here a lot?"

"Sometimes," Jake replied with a small smile. "When I'm trying to quiet my head."

Dillon nodded. "Yeah... it helps." He hesitated, then added, "You wanna be alone?"

"No," Jake said gently, walking to the porch swing and tapping the open space beside him. "Come join me."

They sat in silence for a while — not talking, not needing to. Just swaying.

Then Dillon spoke. His voice was soft, but steady.
"So I wanted to thank you."

Jake turned slightly. "For what?"

"For coming. For making Mom smile again. For listening... you know, for all of it."

Jake didn't answer right away. His throat tightened.

When he finally looked at Dillon, he saw it:
Not just the kid who had lost his father.
Not just the son of the woman he loved.

But a boy – *choosing* him.
Choosing to let him in.

"You're welcome," Jake said, his voice low.

And for the first time in a long time, he didn't feel like a man bracing for the worst.
He felt like a man *building* something better.

Chapter Twenty-Nine

THE GOODBYE

Rainey

The cemetery was quiet.
Still in the way that only sacred places could be.

No wind. No birdsong. Just the soft crunch of leaves beneath her boots as she walked between rows of headstones, one hand clutching the small bouquet she'd arranged that morning: white lilies, blue forget-me-nots, and a single yellow rose — the kind Shane used to leave on her nightstand when he'd travel abroad.

Jake and Dillon waited in the car.

She hadn't asked them to.

They just knew.

This part... she needed to do alone.

The farther she walked, the more the world around her began to fall away — the distant hum of a passing truck, the rhythmic rustle of trees, even the anxious flutter in her chest. All of it softened, until all that remained was the dull thud of her heartbeat, steady but full.

She reached Shane's grave slowly.

The headstone was simple. Clean. Familiar now, but still unkind. She didn't visit often — not because she didn't love him, but because sometimes, being here made it harder to pretend was gone forever.

But today wasn't about pretending.

Today was about truth.

She knelt down now, the cold seeping through the denim at her knees, and placed the flowers at the base of the stone. Her fingers brushed its edge — smooth and solid, like him.

SHANE DEMARCO
Loving Husband. Devoted Father.
Forever Loved

Rainey exhaled.

"I'm here," she whispered. Her voice didn't shake — it landed, grounded and sure.

Her eyes brimmed, but the tears didn't spill.

"I love you," she said. "I'll love you always."

A silence followed.
Not empty.
Holy.

"Jake," she said softly, "He's strong. Quiet. He's been through hell, but he still wants to protect what's good. He loves me. He loves Dillon. He needs us as much as we need him."

The words hung in the air like incense.

She closed her eyes.

"I didn't expect it," she admitted. "Didn't expect to feel anything good again after...you left."

Her voice wavered now.

"But we've been hurting for so long."

> *It was storming — one of those southern spring storms with thunder that rattled the windows and wind that howled like it was mourning something. Dillon was about four and terrified, crawling into their bed with his stuffed teddy bear and trembling lip.*
>
> *Shane pulled him between them and told stories — legends. He made up a tale about thunder being two angels bowling in heaven,*

and how every strike meant the world was safe another day. He said when you're scared or in pain, just call on the angels.

"I don't want to let you go," she said. "That's the part I couldn't say out loud."

The breeze picked up then — not a gust, not a chill, but a gentle movement that seemed to pass through her *from within.*

She stilled.

It wasn't just the wind. It felt... familiar.

A presence.

"I think you'd like him," she said.

> *Her hand reached into her coat pocket and pulled out a folded piece of paper — one she'd written and rewritten many times over the past month. She laid it gently against the flowers. A letter. A tribute to their love and expression of gratitude, similar to the one he'd written her before their vows at sunset on that perfect October evening on the Bahamas beach.*
>
> *The night before their wedding, she'd had a panic attack. She'd never told anyone — not even her mother. She had woken up at 2:13 a.m. with her heart pounding and a suffocating weight in her chest. Shane found her curled on the bathroom floor, naked beneath her robe. He sat down next to her on the cold tile and held her hand until her breathing slowed.*
>
> *"You're stronger than you believe," he whispered. "I'll be here for you always – even in those times when I can't be right beside you."*

Her chest ached. But not the way it used to.

This ache was full. Human. *Alive.*

She stood slowly. Not rushed. Not burdened.

"I'll keep you with me always, Shane," she said. "You'll always be a part of me and Dillon."

She turned toward the car.

Jake was at the driver's seat, one hand on the wheel, the other resting gently behind Dillon's neck. Neither of them said a word as she approached. But both of them looked up with eyes that didn't ask questions.

She opened the door. Sat down.

Jake didn't speak.

He just reached over and wrapped his fingers around hers.

And Rainey knew:
She wasn't leaving Shane behind.
She was walking toward something new.

Jake

The house was warmer than usual that night.

Not just from the fire or the heat from the stove — but from *her*. The way she moved through the rooms, light and deliberate. No longer suspended between past and future, but fully here.

He had always thought healing would come with fanfare — some big revelation, a release of years of pain in a single breath.

But it came quieter than that.

It came in the way she reached for his hand without looking.

The way she laughed softly when Dillon explained his coding project with wild hand gestures.

The way she sat beside him on the porch, wrapped in a blanket, eyes closed, simply breathing.

She hadn't told him what she'd said at Shane's grave.

She didn't need to.

Dillon

He sat on the floor in front of the fireplace, laptop open, muttering to himself as he coded something with the intensity of a man trying to fix the world one line at a time.

Jake was seasoning steaks in the kitchen, halfheartedly watching a football game on the television in the empty game room attached.

Rainey curled up on the living room couch, warm cocoa in hand, bare feet tucked beneath her.

No one spoke for a while.

The house was finally...*quiet.*

Not the kind you fear. Not the kind that makes you crave noise.

Comfortable.

Later, as the sun dipped behind the trees and the fire crackled low, Dillon handed Jake a small circuit board wrapped in paper.

"What's this?" Jake asked.

"A part I didn't use. From the build we worked on," Dillon said. "Thought you could keep it. Since you helped. Maybe we can do something with it later down the road."

Jake turned the piece over in his hands. It was small. Crude. But perfect.

He nodded slowly, throat tight.

"Thanks, Dillon." he said. "I'd like that."

And that moment etched itself deeper into Jake's soul than anything he'd experienced.

Jake & Rainey

That night, Rainey lay tangled in Jake's arms. Her head rested on his chest, her breath syncing with the slow rise and fall of his body.

"I never thought it would feel like this again," she whispered.

Jake traced his fingers along her spine. "Like what?"

"Home."

He didn't speak.

He just kissed the top of her head and held her tighter.

Outside, the porch light clicked off. Inside, the house settled — floorboards creaking softly, night wrapping around them like a promise.

No fear.
No haunting.

Just peace.

Chapter Thirty

THE REMAINS

Rainey

It rained overnight. Just enough to gloss the world in silver and wake the scent of cedar from the trees.

By morning, the house was quiet.

Not the hollow kind. Not the kind she used to brace against after Shane died — the kind that pressed into her ribs and echoed back all the things she had lost.

This quiet was full.

The kettle clicked off in the kitchen. A low thrum from Dillon's laptop hummed down the hallway. Somewhere outside, a bird called once and then went still — as if even nature didn't want to interrupt the peace settling inside their walls.

Rainey stood barefoot in the kitchen, warming her hands on a mug of cinnamon tea. The steam lifted toward her face like breath from something living.

Jake's boots sat by the door. His jacket, folded neatly on the back of a chair. Dillon's hoodie — always halfway off his body no matter the weather — was draped across the railing.

There were signs of *them* everywhere.

And for the first time in nearly two years, Rainey didn't feel like she was walking through a house haunted by absence.

She was walking through a life that had finally begun.

She moved quietly into the living room, where Jake sat on the floor beside Dillon, helping him rewire something that looked both dangerous and brilliant.

"I said *gently*," Dillon muttered, eyeing Jake's grip on a fragile port.

Jake raised his brow. "You want it soldered or snapped?"

"Can it be both?"

Jake shook his head, grinning. "You're lucky I like you."

"You're lucky I need you," Dillon replied.

Rainey smiled behind the rim of her mug, unnoticed for now.

She didn't need to join them.

This moment belonged to *them*.

After breakfast — thick French toast, crisp bacon, laughter at Dillon's unbrushed hair and Jake's failed attempt to flip a piece of toast with a spoon — Rainey stepped out onto the porch with a blanket and a book she wouldn't open.

She curled into the old wicker chair and just... existed.

The sun pushed through a veil of clouds, soft and golden.

Jake stepped out after a few minutes, holding two cups of coffee — hers with just enough cream, his black as always. He handed hers off and sat on the steps beneath her, elbows resting on his knees.

No conversation.
No tension.
Just breath and wood and warm light.

"You know," Jake said eventually, voice low, "I always thought peace was something I'd have to earn through pain."

Rainey looked down at him. "And now?"

He nodded, thoughtful. "I think peace is something you choose to stop running from."

She reached down, threading her fingers through his hair.

Jake closed his eyes.

That was his answer.

Later that day, Rainey moved through the house as though the air had changed. As though something about this morning had carved new space in her chest.

She noticed things now she hadn't before.

The way Dillon muttered full conversations under his breath while coding.

The way Jake always stood between her and the front door, like some instinct in him couldn't relax unless he was guarding.

The way the three of them, without trying, had begun to sync.

It wasn't fast.

It wasn't fireworks.

It was *anchoring*.

And it felt more sacred than anything she'd known.

Jake

He stood in the hallway holding a small black-and-white photo.

Shane.

Younger, smiling, one arm wrapped around a very pregnant Rainey in a sunlit kitchen. She looked radiant. Unaware of the camera. The kind of joy that couldn't be performed — only captured.

Jake stared at it for a long time.

Not with jealousy.
But with reverence.

He walked into the living room and placed the photo in a narrow wooden frame.

Then — quietly, without ceremony — he set it on the shelf beside the others: Dillon at the beach, Rainey reading under a tree, a candid shot Jake had taken of her laughing in the kitchen last week.

Not behind them.
Not separate.

Among them.

Rainey passed through the room moments later.

She paused, eyes catching the new frame.

Her breath caught.

She nodded. "Thank you."

He shrugged, but the moment had gravity.

"He's part of us," Jake said. "Of course he belongs there."

And just like that — without needing to declare or define it — she knew Jake had just given her the final piece of permission her heart needed.

Dillon

They didn't do anything particularly special that evening.

Jake made spaghetti.

Dillon set the table.

Rainey played music — not classical or jazz this time, but an old acoustic playlist they'd once danced to in the living room before one of Shane's trips.

After dinner, they stayed at the table longer than usual.

No one checked their phone.

Jake shared stories from his rookie days — none too dark, just the absurd ones. Like getting locked inside a storage hold with a panicked labrador for two hours. And the dog had diarrhea.

Rainey laughed so hard she snorted. Dillon dropped his fork in disbelief.

It wasn't until much later — when the kitchen was clean, and the house quieted again — that Dillon noticed the photo Jake had placed on the shelf. He knew it was Jake because he'd made a passing comment about the empty frame a day earlier.

He didn't say anything, but he felt *everything* in that moment.

> *Shane's funeral. Random photos of his dad — some from childhood, others a testimony to their family — carefully framed and arranged around the casket like pieces of a life too big to hold. The blurred memory flashes of his mom afterward – moving through the quiet like a ghost, collecting each one as if they were sacred artifacts.*
>
> *Her cries. Her knees buckling in the living room. A frame slipping from her hands. Glass shattering across the floor. A photo torn.*
>
> *And that frame – empty. A cold and silent reminder that sat untouched for the next two years.*

Rainey

The wind picked up.
Branches scratched gently against the roof like the whisper of memory. The fire in the hearth crackled softly, reduced now to embers, glowing low and warm.

Rainey sat at the edge of the bed, slowly brushing her hair, each stroke a ritual, a reclaiming. Her reflection in the mirror wasn't the same woman who had once knelt beside her dying husband, or the one who had drifted through grief like a shadow with no destination.

She saw the wife who had loved with her whole heart — who had memorized his laugh, his silences, his every little habit — and then watched him slip away in a moment that fractured time.
She saw the mother who had crumbled beneath the weight of unspeakable loss — and still rose, day after day, because her son needed someone to believe the world could be safe again.

She had learned to smile again, not because the pain had faded, but because there was no undoing what had been lost — and no life waiting for her in the past.
She had been emptied.
Shaken.
Changed.

But she was still here.
And somehow, she was more than what she had lost.
There was direction in her stillness now. A quiet certainty in the rhythm of her breath.
She was no longer just surviving.

She was living.
And her life — this life — had purpose and value again.

Jake

Jake stood by the window, broad and still, his silhouette carved against the fading twilight. One hand rested on the cool glass, his fingers spread wide, as if grounding himself between the world outside and the one he'd finally stepped into.

The sky beyond had begun to darken, deep blue melting into black, stars surfacing slowly — one by one — like truths too long buried. He wasn't scanning the horizon for movement. He wasn't watching for threats, or waiting for the next mission, the next flight, the next fight.

He was just... watching.

And for a man who had lived most of his life in motion, who'd trained himself to always be a step ahead of what might go wrong — the stillness was almost reverent.

This wasn't a place he'd landed.
It was a place he'd *chosen*.

There was Rainey's quiet strength in the next room.
The echo of Dillon's soft laughter downstairs.
The faint smell of her lotion lingering in the air, mixed with sunrise and birdsong.

And he realized something — something small but holy:
He *wanted* to be a good man in this house.
Not just a protector. Not just a provider.
But a presence.

He wanted to be the reason Rainey felt safe enough to dream again.
To believe that love could show up quietly, without drama or

destruction — just with hands that hold and eyes that stay.
He wanted to show Dillon not all scars meant something was broken beyond repair.
Even warriors could be gentle. Weary hearts could learn to rest.

And beneath that, quieter still, was the ache he carried for his own children — all grown now, scattered – like his past.
He had missed too much.
Not out of neglect, but out of necessity — a life that kept him moving, kept him surviving, while moments slipped away like sand through fingers.
He would never get all that time back.

But maybe he could give something better now.

To Rainey.
To Dillon.
To himself.

Maybe he could still be a father in the ways that mattered — not just by blood, but by choice.
By listening. By staying. By showing up for someone else's boy and letting that choice redeem something of his own.

His chest ached, but not with grief this time.
With hope. A deep, unfamiliar longing to live a life that meant something — not in medals or missions, but in the simple, sacred weight of belonging.

And as the stars bloomed brighter above him, Jake didn't move.
Didn't speak.

Because for the first time in as long as he could remember,
he didn't have to run — from failure, from loss, from the ache of all the ways life had come up short.
And he didn't have to hide — behind duty, behind distance, behind the armor he wore so well it nearly became his skin.

There was nothing to escape here.
No mask to wear.
No war to prepare for.

Just a woman who saw the man he was — and the man he was still trying to become.
A boy who didn't flinch when he reached out.
A life that didn't demand he prove himself, only that he be present.

He had something worth standing still for.
And for once, staying felt like strength —
not surrender.

Dillon

Behind them, in the quiet living room, Dillon curled into Shane's old reclining chair — the one no one had dared to sit in for two long years. It had become something sacred in its stillness, a monument to absence. Rainey had vacuumed around it, dusted the arms gently as if afraid too much pressure might erase what remained. Even Jake, instinctively respectful, had never once looked at it like something he could occupy.

It was more than a chair. It was a tether. A place where Shane's body had rested at the end of every long day, where he'd laughed at movies, read to Dillon, fallen asleep with the TV remote in hand. His scent had long since faded, but the outline of him remained — permanent, invisible, unshakable.

And yet, tonight, Dillon walked toward it without hesitation.

Not because he'd forgotten.
But because he remembered.
And for the first time, the memory felt like a gift he could carry — not a weight he needed to outrun.

He didn't ask for permission. He didn't pause to see if she'd stop him.
He just folded himself into the seat with a quiet reverence — as if honoring his father not by preserving the emptiness, but by allowing something living to exist in that space again.

The chair didn't reject him.
It accepted him.
As if it, too, had been waiting.

And in that moment, it held something new: not the echo of Shane's absence, but the weight of a boy becoming. A boy who had lived through the fire and was still standing. A boy who would carry his father in his heart, not in the empty rooms of a house.

A quiet kind of release.
An unspoken permission to go on.

Jake & Rainey & Dillon

Morning came quietly.
No fanfare. No breaking dawn. Just a soft arrival — like healing itself.
The sun climbed in slow and golden, sifting through sheer white curtains, casting gentle light across wooden floors and quiet rooms. Outside the kitchen window, hummingbirds danced around the feeder, wings flitting in and out like tiny messengers.

Dillon sat cross-legged on the porch swing, a blanket wrapped around his shoulders, a steaming mug of hot chocolate in one hand, and his laptop balanced on his knees. He was writing something.
Or maybe just reflecting.
But his face was calm. Open.
Whole.

Inside, Jake stirred oatmeal in a dented old pot, humming a tune low in his throat — a melody Rainey didn't recognize, but one that made her smile anyway.
His sleeves were rolled up.
His movements were slow and careful, as if he was learning what it meant to stay.

A breeze wandered through the open window, soft and clean, carrying with it the scent of earth and new light. Rainey closed her eyes as it brushed against her skin — not just a touch of air, but something deeper and spiritual. Like the world itself was exhaling a gentle sigh. And for the first time in a long time, she let herself consume it — fully, freely, without fear.

She drew in a deep breath — slow and steady.
She didn't ache.

She didn't mourn.
She didn't brace.

She breathed in peace.

Not out of longing.
Not out of grief.
But out of gratitude.

They hadn't escaped the past.
They hadn't buried it.
They hadn't even fixed it.

But they had learned to carry it — gently, together.
In shared laughter that came easier now.
In footsteps across old wood floors that no longer echoed with emptiness.
In a boy's voice rising with confidence.
In the way Jake's hand would rest on Rainey's back as he passed behind her, grounding her without a word.
In silent glances that said: *I'm here.*
In long walks where they often talked about Shane — but still felt his presence in the rustling trees and remembered paths when they didn't.

Love had not replaced grief.
It hadn't erased it.

It had absorbed it.
Held it.
And made space around it — space for warmth, for laughter, for morning light and the hush of evening skies fading into dusk.
Space for memories that didn't cut.
For new ones that didn't have to compete.

And in that space... they lived.

Because when love remains, it doesn't haunt you like a ghost.
It doesn't ask you to forget.
It becomes something quieter.

It doesn't deny the darkness.

It's the light that leads you home.

ABOUT THE AUTHOR

RHONDA DIMARTINO

When my husband passed away, I didn't just lose him—I lost myself for a very long time. My son and I faced a grief that felt unbearable, and for years, I could not find the strength to give voice to the story that lived inside me. In those years, survival meant nothing more than breathing, functioning, and learning to exist in a world I no longer recognized.

It took time—years of healing, stumbling, and slowly rebuilding—to finally put these words on paper. This story is my testament to the resilience of love, the endurance of memory, and the truth that even after loss, life can surprise us with grace and new beginnings. This book—inspired by our journey—was born from both devastation and resilience, and it stands as my reminder that even in the shadows, love remains.

My greatest wish is that in these words, others who have known grief will find comfort, inspiration, and the reminder that you never stop loving the one you lost— love is not replaced—it expands. Life can surprise us with grace and new beginnings. It is possible to allow yourself to heal, to hope, and to open your heart to love again, and it is possible love can return in a new and beautiful way.

When Love Remains *is the first in a forthcoming series — a hauntingly romantic and emotionally charged journey into what it means to love again after devastating loss. Born in silence, shaped by grief, and anchored in surrender, this story doesn't just speak to the heart — it awakens the senses. Part love story, part reckoning, part revival, it is more than fiction. It is a mirror to the author's own transformation — and only the beginning.*

The heart of the story is still unfolding.